TORN

TORN

Stephanie Guerra

Marshall Cavendish

Other Marshall Cavendish Offices: Marshall Cavendish International (Asia) Private Limited, 1 New Industrial Road, Singapore 536196 • Marshall Cavendish International (Thailand) Co Ltd. 253 Asoke, 12th Flr, Sukhumvit 21 Road, Klongtoey Nua, Wattana, Bangkok 10110, Thailand • Marshall Cavendish (Malaysia) Sdn Bhd, Times Subang, Lot 46, Subang Hi-Tech Industrial Park, Batu Tiga, 40000 Shah Alam, Selangor Darul Ehsan, Malaysia

Marshall Cavendish is a trademark of Times Publishing Limited

Library of Congress Cataloging-in-Publication Data
Guerra, Stephanie.
Torn / by Stephanie Guerra.
p. cm.
Summary: High school senior Estelle Chavez's life in South Bend, Indiana, centers on helping her mother raise her younger brother and sister, AP classes, and soccer until a new student, Ruby, draws her into a friendship that includes sneaking out of the house, dating college boys, and worse.
ISBN 978-0-7614-6272-9 (hardcover) — ISBN 978-0-7614-6273-6 (ebook)
[1. Conduct of life—Fiction. 2. Best friends—Fiction. 3. Friendship—Fiction. 4. High schools—Fiction. 5. Schools—Fiction. 6. Single-parent families—Fiction. 7. Family life—Indiana—Fiction. 8. Indiana—Fiction.] I. Title.
PZ7.G9366Tor 2012
[Fic]—dc23
2011025229

Book design by Becky Terhune
Editor: Marilyn Brigham

Printed in China (E)
First edition
10 9 8 7 6 5 4 3 2 1

mc Marshall Cavendish

For Fonch.
Thank you for
all the memories.

Chapter One

Ruby Caroline put to shame every other grand entrance I'd seen in my life.

It was the third week of my senior year and I was in first-period AP English, staring at Mrs. Leland and wondering how a lady so pretty could look so much like a fullback from the neck down. She was talking essay structure, and most of us were already tuning her out. We'd been getting As on essays since elementary school and were pretty sure we'd keep getting them.

Then the show started.

Wham! The door flew open. A gorgeous girl wearing a Band-Aid of a skirt and a clingy, low-cut shirt stalked in. She slammed her bag on an empty desk. "I can't believe this place," she snarled. With quick, angry hands she gathered her hair—long, dyed reddish blond with split ends, but somehow sexy—on top of her head and snapped it into a messy bun with a plastic clip. She sat down hard. We all stared.

"You must be Ruby," said Mrs. Leland.

"Yeah."

"You seem a little upset. Did something happen that you'd like to share?" Mrs. Leland's voice had softened and lowered. She was one of those touchy-feely teachers.

"That Gestapo hall monitor is on a power trip. She said my shirt is against the dress code, and she tried to make me wear this piece of crap." Ruby pointed to a wad of yellow fabric in her bag. "I think she's just pissed because she's too fat to fit into anything that's not a tent."

I saw Lisa Holmes, student body vice president, exchange glances with Rhetta Nakamura, reigning cheerleader. The message was clear: This would be a girl to hate.

Mrs. Leland clucked gently. "We do have a dress code, but I'm sorry you had that experience on your first day here. It probably didn't feel very welcoming."

"Whatever," said Ruby.

Mrs. Leland glanced around the classroom. "Everyone, this is Ruby Caroline. She just moved here from Utah." That surprised me. For someone from Utah, Ruby looked like the photo negative of a Mormon.

"Would everyone mind introducing themselves? We'll just go around the room, and you can tell us your name and one of your favorite books." Mrs. Leland's eyes came to rest on me. "Estelle? Would you like to start?"

"Um, Stella Chavez. *Anna Karenina*," I said. And we kept going around the room.

Like the rest of the class, I couldn't take my eyes off Ruby. I kept stealing glances, checking the details: scuffed three-inch heels, a tan to die for, a couple of scars on her knees, glossy pink lips, liquid eyeliner, and startling, contemptuous green eyes.

She caught me looking. "What?" she said loudly, staring back.

Mrs. Leland's head swiveled. "Ruby? Let's not talk in class, please, dear."

Ruby sighed.

After that I kept my eyes to myself. But I was replaying her entrance in my head and wondering: who *was* this girl? Or maybe: who did she think she was?

After English I headed to history, then precalc, then lunch. Lunch had been a little loose ended since my best friend, Elsa, moved away the past spring. Without her our group felt lopsided. But Beth and Christine and I still followed our routine from junior year, buying sodas and eating together in the soccer field.

Except today Ruby caught me halfway to the soda machine.

"Hey, Estelle," she said, falling into step beside me.

I looked at her, shocked that she remembered my name. "Hey."

"You got a car?"

I nodded.

"Want to go to lunch?"

"Okay." The funny thing is, I didn't even think about saying no, or bringing up the fact that we only get two off-campus lunch passes each month and I'd already used up one of them. I just led the way through the parking lot to my slightly-better-than-scrap-metal Mazda, swept a pile of papers off the front seat, and started the engine.

Ruby rolled down her window and pulled a pack of cigarettes

from her bag, smacking the bottom to settle the tobacco. She flicked a lighter and took a long drag. A wreath of smoke curled from her nostrils. "Want one?" She held out the box to me, but I shook my head. Cigarettes were once-in-a-while treats at parties, nothing I wanted to get into every day.

We hit the exit station, and the gate attendant asked for our names and IDs.

"Estelle Chavez," I told him, holding out my license.

"Brianna Pippin," said Ruby.

"ID?" the attendant prompted.

"My purse got stolen last week," Ruby said, keeping her cigarette hand out the window.

"I'm sorry, miss, I need to see some picture identification."

Ruby peered past me at the man's name tag. "Garrett? Can you do me a favor and just let it go this time? It really sucked to get my purse stolen."

The attendant sighed and waved us through, scribbling our names on his roster.

I looked at Ruby. "Brianna is going to freak when she finds out somebody used her pass." I didn't mention that Brianna and I were friends on the soccer team.

"So?" Ruby closed her eyes and took another drag. "She was a bitch to me in Spanish. You got a smoothie place around here?"

"There's a Jamba Juice in the strip mall down the road. You want to go there?"

"Yeah, that sounds good." Ruby sighed, a heavy, theatrical sigh. "This place. It's killing me."

"Already? You just got here."

"That's what I'm scared of. It's only been two days, and I think I'm going to lose my mind."

"Utah was so much better?"

"No," Ruby snorted. "Now that you mention it."

"Well, it's not so terrible here. You'll get used to it," I said as reassuringly as I could.

It was true: South Bend wasn't bad. We were two hours outside of Chicago, population a hundred thousand or so. It had a small-town feel but wasn't as claustrophobic as some of the nearby farm towns. And we had Notre Dame. The university was our big claim to fame, bringing in thousands of rich kids, die-hard Catholics, and football fans every year.

We got our smoothies and parked in front of the dollar store. Ruby sipped and smoked, and I stirred my smoothie with a spoon and ate it like ice cream, the way I always did. The whole thing felt a little surreal.

"So what's your story?" Ruby asked.

"My story?"

"Yeah, you know, family, boyfriend, what are you into, blah, blah, blah. And what are you, anyway? Latina? You look like some kind of mix."

I appreciated how straightforward she was, not darting me little looks and trying to guess like most people did. "Well, my dad's Mexican and my mom's Croatian. But my mom's family immigrated here like a hundred years ago, and my dad left when we were little. So we're pretty much white; we just look Mexican."

Ruby exhaled. "Huh. That's interesting. You got a boyfriend?"

I thought of Trevor Dodd, the latest in a line of two-month relationships. He was a jock like me—men's basketball—tall and blond and predictably nice. I always date the nice ones, but things seem to peter out after a couple of months, usually because I get bored. "Kind of."

"What do you mean, 'kind of'? You're obviously not that into him if he's only 'kind of' your boyfriend."

"That's true," I admitted. "What about you?"

"I haven't exactly been here long enough to hook up with anybody. Besides, I don't date high school boys."

From anyone else that would have seemed like bragging, but from Ruby it sounded like plain fact.

"The Notre Dame guys, that's who I'll date," Ruby went on. "I just haven't met the right one yet." She ashed her cigarette. "So are you popular?"

"Am I popular?" I echoed. "Um . . ."

"Be honest. I hate bullshit."

Something inside me relaxed. I like straight talking, maybe because that's how my mom is. It had taken me years to learn that in polite society you should almost never say what you're really thinking or ask what you really want to know. Now here was Ruby, breaking all the rules. I liked it.

"Sort of," I told her. "Not top-tier cheerleader popular, but I play soccer, so I hang out with a lot of the jocks. I'm also in a bunch of AP classes, so I know some nerds and student body people. I kind of fit in with everybody."

"Well, isn't that an enviable position," said Ruby.

"What about you? Who did you hang out with at your old school?"

Ruby gazed at the dashboard for a minute before answering.

"It's a long story." Then she glanced at her naked wrist as if she were checking a watch. "Aren't we going to be late?"

I didn't believe she cared one bit if we were late, but I started the car. Ruby fiddled with the stereo and found a classic rock station playing Pink Floyd. She cranked it up until my poor stereo was crackling with effort, Pink Floyd's depressing moan throbbing in my eardrums: *"Hello, hello, hello, . . . Is there anybody in there? Just nod if you can hear me. Is there anyone at home?"*

Ruby sang along enthusiastically.

When we got back to school she gave me a big smile and hauled her bag over her shoulder. "See you later, alligator."

Then she walked off, not even waiting to find out if I was headed in the same direction, her heels clicking on the concrete. For such a sexy girl, she had an almost-military way of walking: straight and fast, no swing to her hips, shoulders back and head high. I watched her go. Even though all we'd done was get a smoothie, I felt as if I'd had an adventure.

Chapter Two

The next few days I walked extra slowly to the soda machine, but Ruby was never around. I wondered if she'd found somebody else with a car and was going through a roster of other people's names, using up their passes. I wondered why I cared. The only class I had with her was AP English, where she'd alternate between staring off with a vacant expression and voicing loud, sudden opinions in class discussions. Nobody really liked Ruby, but everybody wanted to know more about her.

Christine and Beth were speculating about which crowd she'd fall into—the druggie sluts, they thought. And Trevor, who had chemistry class with her, talked about Ruby in a fascinated way that I didn't like. It was obvious he thought she was hot.

Then, on Thursday night, she called.

"It's for you, Stella," my little brother, Marcus, yelled over the blare of the TV. He was ten, and if he had a lobotomy, they'd find Xbox circuitry instead of a brain.

I grabbed the upstairs extension. Marcus had been known to hang up if I took too long getting to the phone. "Hello?"

"Hey, it's Ruby. From English."

"Hey," I said.

"Listen, what are you doing tonight?"

"Um . . . I don't know."

"Good. Let's go out. Can you pick me up at ten? I live by the Notre Dame campus."

"I don't think I can," I said, trying to hide my surprise. "My curfew is nine on weeknights."

"Your *curfew?*" There was a long pause. "Well, just sneak out then."

I gave a weak laugh. "It's not that easy."

"Why? Is the door right by your parents' room or something? You should try a window."

I thought about it. The door was nowhere near my mom's room. It wouldn't be hard to sneak out at all, actually. The thing was, I'd never done it before. But I would have died before admitting that to Ruby. "Okay. Where do you live?" I asked finally.

"Corner of Juniper and Fourteenth. The green house with the gables. Dress cute."

She hung up before I could ask where we were going. I stared at the phone for a second, like maybe it could give me some answers. For example, how had she gotten my phone number? And what on earth was there to do on a Thursday night in a town as small as South Bend?

If Ruby had known how much trouble those two words—*dress cute*—were going to cause me, she might not have said them. I spent an hour obsessing in my bedroom, trying on everything in my closet. Did she mean casual cute? Dressy cute? Sexy cute?

Finally, my sister, Jackie, poked her head in the doorway and said, "Are you getting ready for the prom or something?" Jackie was thirteen and the biggest know-it-all you ever met. You know the stereotype of the Latina teenybopper with coon eyes and dagger nails and bloodred lips? That was Jackie. Except somehow she still looked good. And she actually had some brain cells, according to her report cards.

"None of your business," I told her.

"You're going somewhere."

"No, I'm not. Can I have some privacy, please?" I pushed the door shut.

I needed to pick something quick, before Jackie got even more suspicious. I settled on one of my staple outfits: my favorite jeans and a black wraparound shirt that made me look a little fuller up top. I went through the charade of dinner with Mom, Jackie, and Marcus and faked an early bedtime. My palms were moist by nine o'clock.

Here was the thing. My mom trusted me. I trusted my mom. It had been just the two of us trying to raise Jackie and Marcus since my loser dad bailed out; and even though I probably wasn't as good as an actual adult male, I was a big help. My mom had a few ground rules—normal stuff like curfew—but mostly she let me do what I wanted.

We were a team.

Sneaking out was something a rat like my dad would do, not me. Except that night I went ahead and did it. I swear, Ruby was like the Pied Piper or something.

I drove down the quiet streets the few miles to her house and pulled up to the curb, cutting the engine. It was a pretty house, one of those old ramshackle Victorians with loads of personality. There was a crooked little gate out front, and all the downstairs windows were glowing.

That wasn't a good sign; it meant Ruby's parents were probably up. I waited; but the lights stayed on, and I started thinking of more and more reasons why I should turn around and go home. I could even stop at 7-Eleven and pick up some tampons, so if Mom woke up when I came in, I could tell her I had to run out on an emergency errand.

I stuck the key back in the ignition and was just about to leave when Ruby's door swung open. I could see her silhouetted on the steps. She peered at me and then started down the walkway to the street.

I rolled down the window.

"What are you doing?" Ruby sounded amused. "Were you waiting out here? Why didn't you knock on the door or beep or something?"

I shrugged, embarrassed. "All the lights were on, so I figured your parents were up."

"My . . . mom is up." The way Ruby said *mom* was a little strange. "But she doesn't care that we're going out. You want to meet her?"

I nodded and got out of the car to follow Ruby inside.

We walked through a foyer filled with moving boxes into a big, empty living room. A thin, dark-haired woman in silky men's pajamas was curled on the couch with a book. When she looked up, I was shocked by how beautiful she was. Her eyes were large and dark, her skin was pale, and she looked almost

Spanish or something. Nothing like Ruby, except for the full lips.

"Gina, this is Estelle. Estelle, Gina."

"Nice to meet you, Mrs. Caroline," I said automatically, thinking how weird it was that Ruby called her mom by her first name. I extended my hand.

"Just Gina is fine." She shook my hand and gave me a once-over. Then she said to Ruby, "Can you pick up some seltzer while you're out?"

"Gina, this is South Bend. Nothing is open past five."

"Actually, Frank's doesn't close until eight," I offered, before I realized that Ruby was being sarcastic.

"I'm sure you can find a twenty-four-hour convenience store." Gina's eyes were already back on her book.

"Come on. I gotta finish getting ready," Ruby told me.

Feeling a little dazed, I trailed behind her to her room. The hall was a mess of half-unpacked boxes, and I caught a glimpse of a bathroom that looked like a ransacked beauty supply store. Ruby's room was the same. Clothes and makeup and aerosol bottles littered the floor. The bed was a bare mattress with a down comforter wadded in one corner. The sweet, hippie smell of incense lingered in the air.

Ruby looked me up and down and shook her head. "No offense, but that isn't going to work. You look like some kind of sorority chick."

I was so stunned I couldn't even be offended. "It's just a black top and jeans!"

"Exactly; boring. Here, good thing you're skinny. You'll probably fit into some of my stuff." Businesslike, Ruby began to pluck through one of the piles on the floor. I was horrified to see sequins, spaghetti straps, and glitter. She shook free a silver tank top, teeny tiny, with ruched sides and a plunging neckline. "This and some heels will spice up those jeans."

"That looks like a stripper top! Where are we going, anyway? It's ten-thirty at night." I was totally weirded out. This was South Bend. There was school tomorrow. And Ruby's model mother was reading on the couch, oblivious as her daughter and a strange friend sifted through nightclub gear on their way out . . . somewhere.

"Sorry, I should have told you. We have a date."

"A *date*?"

"Yeah. Some Notre Dame guys." Ruby unscrewed the cap from a little tube on her dresser and smoothed pink gloss over her lips.

"What are you talking about, a date?"

"What, you don't really like that boyfriend of yours, do you?"

"His name is Trevor. And no, we're not that serious, but—"

"Quit worrying. It'll be fun."

I shook my head, stubborn. "This is crazy. You don't tell me anything, but you expect me to show up this late on a school night and go on some date with you?"

Ruby sized me up with a quick, searching look, and I swear I saw her conclude that I wasn't as malleable as she'd thought. "All right, here's the deal. I met this hot guy, and he wants to hang out tonight. I said I'd bring somebody for his friend."

"You needed a pity date and a ride so you called *me*?"

Ruby flashed a grin. "Well, I wouldn't put it that way, but sort of. I don't know anybody else. And you're pretty."

I grinned back. For some reason I wasn't bothered by the

fact that she was obviously using me, at least now that she was being up front about it. "Fine, but I'm not wearing that thing."

· "Why not? It's hot!" Ruby saw from the look on my face that she wasn't going to win. "Okay, what about this one?" She scooped up another tank top: black, with spangles along the neckline. "Very sexy. Latin lover."

"I'll try it on." I shrugged out of my shirt and tugged the tank top over my head.

Ruby circled me, checking all angles. "Perfect. You'll have to fight him off."

That made me a little nervous. "Who is he, anyway? What's he like?"

"Um . . ." Ruby looked guilty. "I think his name is Mike."

"You haven't met him?"

"Well, no, but my date said he's a really nice guy." She smiled a totally charming, sheepish grin. "Look, I'll make it up to you, okay?"

"Right," I grumbled, but I wasn't really mad. A date with college guys was way better than my usual going-out scene: predictable parties in which everybody I'd known since grade school ended up drunk and puking on one another.

Ruby turned her attention to getting ready, shimmying out of her jeans and sweater and holding up different outfits in the mirror. I tried not to stare. She had a woman's body, not a hint of little-girl anywhere. How did she manage to avoid tan lines?

"What time are we supposed to be there?" I thought to ask.

"Ten."

"But it's almost ten forty-five!"

She gave me a withering look. "Always make them wait." Then she slid into a pair of faux leather pants, a black top, and stiletto boots that would have looked ridiculous on anyone else. On her they looked glam: playful, sexy, eighties glam—retro with a twist. "How do I look?"

"Great." I couldn't even be jealous, the whole getup was so far out of my league.

"Then let's get out of here."

In the car, Ruby lit a cigarette and took a drag. "Down Edison past Grape and right on Mishawaka. They live in some apartments off Mishawaka and Eighth."

"We're going to their house?"

"Where else would we be going this late? Everything is closed except bars, and I figured you wouldn't be able to get in. You don't have an ID, do you?"

"No. Do you?"

"Of course." She sounded offended that I'd asked. "Don't worry. Give me a couple weeks and I'll get you one, too."

I wasn't so sure about that. Matt Connor and David Leahy had the only ID business in town, and their IDs weren't always even good enough for buying beer at the mini-mart, let alone getting into Corby's or Heartland. Still, they ran the scene, unless you could get someone over twenty-one to lend you her license. But if anyone could find another ID source, it would be Ruby.

"I think it's up there on your right. See the brick complex?" Ruby gestured with her cigarette.

I swung into the driveway, winding past the leasing office into a complex of colonial-style apartments. They looked pretty upscale for Mishawaka.

"His parents are loaded," Ruby said, reading my mind. "Go all the way back. It's on the left, I think." She dug in her purse and pulled out a silver cell, dialing quickly. "Sean? We're here. Yeah. Blue car. Okay, see you in a minute." Ruby tucked the phone back in her purse. "Park anywhere. They're coming out to meet us."

Chapter Three

I pulled into a space and cut the motor. I could already see them, two dark figures against the balcony. "Up here!" one of them called, waving.

Ruby took her time, smoothing her hair in the rearview mirror before she got out of the car and sauntered up the steps. I followed, feeling more than a little nervous.

"Hey, Sean." Ruby leaned in to exchange a cheek kiss with a tall man. I couldn't make out his face very well in the dark, but he ushered us inside quickly.

Sean *was* hot. Big and lean and powerfully built, he had short black hair and a serious, manly face that reminded me of some secret agent pretending to keep a low profile. Mike, or whatever his name was, was pretty good-looking himself, though not quite as striking as Sean. He was going on six feet with a stocky build, blond hair, and close-set, intelligent green eyes.

Sean introduced us and did all the hosting things: taking our jackets, showing us the couch. He gestured to an open bottle on the counter. "We were making vodka tonics. Do you want one?" The casual way Sean offered the drinks was the complete opposite of how Trevor or Ben or Casey or any of the high school boys I knew would have acted, showing off the alcohol like it was a big deal, telling war stories about how they tricked the guy at the liquor store counter.

The startling thought occurred to me that Sean might be over twenty-one.

"I'll have one," said Ruby.

Mike glanced at me, and I shook my head. "I'm driving." It was a convenient excuse; I probably wouldn't have wanted to drink even if I didn't have the car. Everything was too strange; and unlike most people, I don't like to drink unless I'm already comfortable.

Mike patted the couch next to him, and I sat down awkwardly, keeping some distance between us. "So, what's your major?" he asked.

My mouth hung open for a second before Ruby rescued me. "She's not in college. We're seniors in high school."

Now it was Mike's turn to gape. He looked at Sean, but Sean was concentrating on pouring tonic into a glass nearly half full with vodka.

"Sean didn't tell you? Is it really such a big deal?" Ruby kept her eyes on Mike, and I could sense him wilting under the pressure.

"Well, no, it's just . . . I was surprised is all." He laughed, shrugging it off.

"How about you? What's your major?" Ruby asked.

"Business."

"Are you a junior like Sean?"

"No, sophomore."

"Ruby, your drink is ready." Sean patted a bar stool at the granite counter in the kitchen. "Come sit with me."

Ruby and Sean were only across the room from Mike and me, but they could have been miles away. The high-backed leather sofa was arranged with a recliner around a giant flat-screen TV; and facing away from the kitchen, it felt as if we were in our own little cocoon.

Mike scooted closer to me. "You have really beautiful eyes, you know that?"

I looked down, embarrassed.

"No, you do. Exotic."

I felt a finger under my chin, and Mike was leaning in, breath tinged with alcohol. I reared back, and Mike jerked away. "Sorry, I didn't mean to . . ."

"That's okay. Look, I don't know what Sean told you, but I didn't come here to hook up with you."

"Yeah, I know," Mike said, his cheeks flushed. I almost felt sorry for him, he looked so ashamed. Truthfully, I wasn't entirely opposed to kissing him; but I was insulted that he tried so fast, as if I were a slut or something.

"So how do you like Notre Dame?" I asked, trying to ease the awkwardness.

"I love it," Mike said quickly. "I played football in high school, and my family is Catholic, so it's kind of a big deal that I'm going here."

"You go to a lot of the football games?"

That was all it took to get him started. He went on about

the latest coach and the tough run of luck the team had over the past few years. He seemed to know all the players by name and practically the last four decades of school football history.

I listened, nodding and saying "uh-huh" and "mm-hmm" at the right moments.

Mike was about the billionth in a line of football-obsessed men I'd known, including my brother, every guy I'd ever dated, and most of my male friends. There was something in the South Bend air that turned perfectly rational human males into screaming, Michigan- and USC-hating, marshmallow-throwing, beer-chugging lunatics. Their brains were like Notre Dame playbooks, memorizing every pass and tackle.

I didn't love it, but I was used to it.

Mike must have appreciated the audience, because after a while he stopped and said, "You know, you're pretty mature for a high school girl."

I laughed. "Is that supposed to be a compliment?"

"Well, yeah."

"Thank you, then." I looked at him mischievously and he grinned—a real grin, not a seductive one like he'd been trying earlier.

"What I mean is, you're pretty cool. Period."

"And mature?"

"And mature."

"You're only saying that because I let you talk about football for an hour straight."

We were both smiling now, and I was pleasantly conscious of the closeness of Mike's arm to my back. Our eyes caught and held. Then the moment was shattered by a *smack*—it had to be a hand on flesh; there was nothing else that sounded like that—and the quick thud of footsteps.

Ruby tore into the living room from somewhere down the hall (I hadn't even realized she'd left the kitchen) and stopped dramatically in front of us. "Estelle, come on. We're leaving."

"What?"

"Let's get out of here." Ruby threw a dark look over her shoulder as Sean emerged from the hall behind her, looking angry and confused.

"Ruby, wait! You can't just go! What the hell?" he said.

I stood, full of awful visions of what might have happened. "Bye," I whispered to Mike, and I gave his hand a squeeze.

"Come on, Estelle." Ruby took my arm and nearly dragged me out the door, clattering down the steps on her high heels.

Her mood was contagious, and I jogged to my car feeling panicky, as if Sean were actually chasing us. I didn't feel safe again until I'd revved the engine and peeled out of the gates down Mishawaka Avenue.

"What happened?" I asked. "Are you okay?"

To my shock, Ruby let out a giggle. "Yeah."

"Why are you laughing? What happened in there?" I could see now that Ruby was perfectly fine, her eyes bright with excitement.

"I had to teach him a lesson." She fished around in her purse for yet another cigarette. I was starting to feel as if I needed one, too. "Look. There are some caveats to dating college guys, especially ones as hot and smart as Sean. They don't take you seriously at first. They think they're slumming even talking to a high school girl. If you let them, they'll have sex with you and never call you again."

My mouth made a small *o* and I snuck a glance at Ruby.

"So you have to *make* them take you seriously," she continued. "That's actually pretty formulaic: you just have to play hard as hell to get. They love it. They come panting like puppies."

"So what was the slap about? Did he try to hook up with you or something?"

Ruby nodded, pleased with herself. "Yeah. We were kissing, and he tried to undo my pants. That one is smooth. He can unbutton things one-handed. That's when I slapped him. You watch: he'll be calling any second now."

Like magic, the phone began to ring from somewhere in the depths of Ruby's purse.

Ruby smiled. "The harder it is to get, the more they want it." She sounded like she was reciting a mantra.

I was transfixed. This strategy was light-years beyond the "tell Katie to tell Brad that I like him" that I was used to. It suddenly made the evenings spent with Christine and Beth and Elsa agonizing over whether or not to call some guy seem unbelievably juvenile.

"That's pretty smart," I admitted. "Are you going to call him back?"

"Of course not. I'll let him call for the next couple days, then I'll answer some time this weekend and let him apologize."

"But what's the point of making him chase you if you're not going to hook up with him?"

Ruby gave me a look like I might be a little slow. "I never said I wouldn't hook up with him. But he needs to want me more than I want him."

I had other questions, but I didn't want to seem too naive.

I looked at the clock on the dash. It was almost one in the morning. A vision of my mom in her gray sweats, pacing the living room confused and worried, flashed into my mind. I sped up and got Ruby home as fast as I could.

"Thanks, Estelle." Ruby scooped up her purse and was halfway out of the car when she asked, "Oh yeah, did you have fun with Mike?"

I had to laugh. "Yeah, we had a good time talking." As she turned away, a thought struck me. "Weren't we supposed to get seltzer for your mom?"

Ruby shrugged. "She won't even remember she asked." Then she shut the door.

Out of habit, I watched Ruby go up the sidewalk. Christine and Beth and I always watched one another into the house when we did late night drop-offs, but I had a feeling Ruby could take care of herself.

I hit the gas and got myself home. The windows were dark, and the back door opened with a squeak that sent my heart rocketing; but nothing happened. I crept to my room, yanking off Ruby's shirt and diving under the covers, not even bothering to scrub off my makeup.

I felt crazy guilty. Mom was in the next room, due to wake up in a couple of hours for her 6 a.m. waitressing shift.

I'll never sneak out again, I promised myself. But even as I thought it, I knew it wasn't true.

Chapter Four

After that night, Ruby officially adopted me. Me and my car, to be more exact. I didn't have to wonder if she'd say hi in AP English or want to eat lunch with me. Suddenly it was a known thing: Ruby and I were tight.

It was mostly her doing.

I wasn't confident enough to call her—I didn't assume we were good friends yet—but she started calling me almost every night. Before long we got to that comfortable stage where you can waste hours talking about nothing.

I gave her a ride home from school a few times, and she always invited me in—and then one day she invited herself to *my* house. It was after school, and she caught up with me in the parking lot. "What are you doing right now?" she asked.

I shrugged. "Just going home."

"Can I come over? I want to see your place."

I couldn't say no. But I was nervous. Now that her mom

had unpacked, her house seriously looked like something out of a magazine.

My house—not so much. Mom and I had given up on "clean" long ago and, at best, were trying for "decent." Taking care of Jackie and Marcus was a full-time job in itself, and we didn't have time for dusting and mopping and detail work. In fact, we were lucky if the laundry got done and there were clean dishes in the cupboards.

I pictured Ruby using the bathroom and being totally grossed out by the dirty sink. Or what if she tried to get a glass of water and it had one of those lipstick prints Jackie left on everything she touched?

I shouldn't have worried.

Ruby walked into my house, found the fridge, and got herself a Diet Coke. Then she collapsed on the couch and announced with honest admiration, "This is so comfortable."

That little comment by itself made our friendship stronger. But even more important was how Ruby reacted to Mom, who got home a little while later. Ruby and I were still on the couch with our drinks, flipping through channels, looking for something decent to watch.

The key turned in the lock, and Mom pushed through, arms heavy with grocery bags.

Ruby got up immediately. "Can I help you with those?"

I looked at her in surprise. She sounded so eager and polite.

"Sure!" said Mom with a smile. She glanced at me, eyebrows raised, as she handed Ruby a few of the bags.

"Oh, sorry," I said. "Mom, this is Ruby. Ruby, this is my mom."

"Nice to meet you, Mrs. Chavez," Ruby said in the same

bright voice, carrying the bags to the kitchen.

Mom got busy putting away the food, and Ruby insisted on helping. She chatted the whole time, asking Mom about her job and telling her about the move from Utah. She told Mom things she hadn't told *me* yet.

I thought Ruby might look down on my mom, or at minimum ignore her. But it was the opposite. Ruby was practically doing cartwheels for her.

I knew then that no matter how beautiful Ruby was, she wasn't stuck up. And she cared enough about me to want to impress my family.

I tried to explain this to Christine and Beth, who thought Ruby was conceited, like people at school were saying. But they weren't buying it.

"Are you having lunch with her *again*?" Christine asked me one day in precalc after I'd been hanging out with Ruby for a few weeks. Her nose wrinkled in distaste.

I shrugged. "Probably."

"Why don't you guys eat with us?"

There was no good answer to that.

Instinctively, I knew Ruby would rather eat by herself than hang out with Christine and Beth. She was territorial, like some kind of big cat, and she had marked me for her own. This thrilled me in a weird way that was impossible to explain. "I don't know. I'll ask her," I said.

"Do you actually like her?" Christine asked.

"No, I hang out with her because I can't stand her."

"Sorry, just asking." Christine rolled her eyes.

Christine and I always had a funny tension between us. We were both the oldest kids in our families, used to being in charge. And Christine had a way of insinuating things that made me crazy. It had been easier when Elsa was around to balance us out with her humor. Now random stuff was starting to annoy me, like the way Christine chewed her food really, really thoroughly and her habit of saving every single receipt. It was probably a good thing we were getting a break from each other.

Beth was wondering about my lunches with Ruby, too. I'd always been closer to Beth than to Christine, and I felt bad when she said, "We've been missing you at lunch."

"I'm just helping Ruby get settled in. She doesn't really know anybody," I explained.

"She seems pretty confident. I bet she could make friends."

"Yeah, probably."

"Well, no pressure, but if you ever want to ask her to eat with us . . ." Beth trailed off, and I felt a pang.

Beth was one of those lovable people without an ounce of mean in her entire body. Her clear brown eyes and bad perm and downhill battle with pastries were so dear and familiar. I loved Beth's bad habits: the nervous twisting of her ring, the way she chewed up all her pencils.

"I will. I'll see if she wants to," I said. But I didn't sound convincing even to my own ears.

That was nowhere near the end of it, though. Rhetta Nakamura, Emma Hausbeck, and the other cheerleaders started paying more attention to me because I was their only channel to the mysterious Ruby.

In our school, the cheerleaders were a funny thing. Elsa and Christine and Beth and I had discussed it many times: generally, except for Lisa Holmes, they weren't that pretty.

Certainly not the pack of stick-thin, balloon-boobed blondes that everybody thinks of when you say "cheerleader." Arie's nose was too big for her face, Melanie was on the heavy side, Emma's body seemed pointy and wrong, Rhetta *looked* mean, and Stacy was awfully gummy when she smiled. And yet they were top-tier popular and sought after by boys like Levi Hanks and Matt Sanders.

I guess just being a cheerleader has so much social power that it makes up for all kinds of problems. That, and spending ridiculous amounts of money on hair and makeup.

Anyway, there were enough rumors about Ruby to start a blog, and everybody thought I had the answers.

"Does Ruby really live by herself?" Brianna asked me at soccer practice.

"Does she like Todd Mackey?" Arie wanted to know.

"Does Ruby know where to get E?" Fern Samuels asked me furtively at break.

The guys had something else on their minds. "Is Ruby hooking up with anybody?" Luke Burrell asked, with Matt Sanders and Levi Hanks standing by, ears pricked.

"Is Ruby going with somebody to Sadie Hawkins?" Brent Tano whispered in biology.

"They're saying Ruby got together with, like, half the Saint Joe's football team," Trevor, my sort-of boyfriend, told me one afternoon after school as we were waiting for our teams to practice. "They're making bets on who can do her first."

I looked at him coldly. "Ruby wouldn't have sex with some stupid high school guy for a million dollars. Tell your friends to quit spreading rumors."

Trevor put up his hands in mock defense. "Okay, jeez. I

was just asking." Then he frowned as the comment sank in. "*Stupid high school guy?* What's that supposed to mean?"

"Never mind." I was sick of all the gossip and lies. High school guys *were* stupid; I just hadn't realized it before. A familiar feeling was bubbling up: the breakup feeling. It was the point when the scales tipped so far toward apathy that I knew the relationship was doomed.

I sighed. "Trevor, we need to talk."

With a beginning like that, he had to know what was coming. "You know, you've been acting like a bitch ever since you started hanging out with that girl," he said defensively.

That made it easier for me. "Maybe we should just be friends."

It was the biggest cliché in the universe, and Trevor knew it. "Whatever, Stella. I guess that's all we really were, anyway." He gave me a look of disgust and walked off.

That Friday Ruby asked me to go to Chicago. It was after school, and we were on our way to the parking lot. I had started giving Ruby a ride home after school on days when I didn't have soccer practice and Sean couldn't pick her up. "You want to go to Chicago tomorrow?" she said out of the blue.

"Chicago?" I echoed.

"Yeah, Chicago. The big city across the Illinois border?"

"That's kind of . . . far." I didn't want to tell the truth, which was that my mom wouldn't like it.

"Far! It's two hours."

"What do you want to do in Chicago?"

"Snort coke through dollar bills and dance in G-strings for hot stockbrokers, what do you think?"

I looked at Ruby to make sure she was kidding, and she roared with laughter. "Stella, you are so gullible! You should see your face! We're just going shopping, okay? I need some new stuff."

"*You* need new stuff?" I had seen her room a number of times now, and she had more clothes than your average mall.

"Yeah. Sean is a preppy rich boy. If I want to get written into the will, I have to start looking the part."

"I think Sean likes you just fine the way you are." As Ruby had predicted, Sean had begged and apologized until she went out with him again. Now they were evolving into what looked to me like a couple.

"He still doesn't take me seriously." Ruby plucked at her tight, shimmery shirt with distaste. "This looks young."

"You *are* young."

"Yeah, well, I don't have to look it. Donna Karan, that's what I'm thinking. Armani."

"That stuff is, like, a million dollars."

Ruby poked me in the side. "Quit being such a downer, okay? What time should we leave tomorrow?"

I did the mental math, a complicated equation of lies and drive times and potential traffic. "Noon?"

I was rewarded with a giant smile.

Still, it didn't make up for the charade I had to go through with my mom that night. "You're spending the *whole day* with Ruby," my mom repeated, sudsing up dishes in the sink. Her curly gray hair was extrawild, frizzing above the ears like a mad scientist's.

"Yeah. Is that okay?"

"Sure, Stel, you're a big girl. You can choose your friends. But

I don't know what I think about Ruby yet. She's a little smooth for my liking."

I knew exactly what Mom was talking about, but I acted offended. "You only met her once. She's a really nice girl. Just because she's pretty doesn't mean she's *smooth*."

"Whatever you say. What are you girls going to do?"

"I don't know, hang out." I was purposely vague, trying to avoid a lie.

"Fine, as long as you're home to help me get Marcus fed and in bed. I have to work a double tomorrow, and Jackie is going to her friend's house to study." Mom dried her hands on a dish towel and swept her stubborn frizz back from her face with a sigh. Her blue eyes looked tired.

"You have to get Bill to stop giving you doubles. It's ridiculous."

"Yeah, well, that's life." Mom patted me on my shoulder. "I sleep every other night. . . ."

"And eat ramen noodles three meals a day just to feed your kids," I finished. It was an inside joke based on some guilt trip my grandpa used to give her.

My mom was an easy person to love. Down to earth, relaxed, hardworking, and totally committed to me and Jackie and Marcus. I'd always counted her as one of my best friends. It bothered me that it was getting easier to lie to her, or leave her out of the loop.

"Just be careful with Ruby. You don't know her very well yet," Mom said over her shoulder.

"Okay, overprotective one." I softened it with a quick hug, relieved she hadn't asked any more questions.

✳

Ruby was chatty in the car the next morning. She brought a bottle of red nail polish and was trying to give herself a pedicure on my dashboard while we drove. I kept glancing at her, sure the polish would topple and ruin my front seat.

"Would you relax?" Ruby giggled. "Don't you know by now I *don't . . . make . . . mistakes?*" She jabbed a dot of polish on a toe for emphasis with each word.

"Just don't spill it," I muttered.

"So what's up with your friends? How come they keep giving me dirty looks at school?"

"Who does?"

"I don't know their names. The fat blonde. And the one who looks like a man."

"Beth and Christine," I said stiffly.

"Yeah, them. Not that they're alone." Ruby rolled her eyes. "I'm so sick of high school. It's such an incestuous, viperous little gossip pit."

I couldn't help giggling. Ruby had a knack for putting things exactly the right way. "Everybody's just curious about you. You don't talk to anyone, so of course they think you're stuck up."

Ruby looked pleased.

"Did you know the guys are laying bets on who'll get to sleep with you first?"

She howled with laughter. "Oh, boy. That's good. How much are they betting; do you know?"

"No, I didn't ask," I told her.

"Tell them for a million they can have me, okay?"

I looked at her sideways, and she exploded into laughter again.

The rest of the car ride passed quickly, until we found

ourselves fighting traffic on the crowded streets of Chicago's shopping district. I hated the city traffic; it swelled around us like a powerful tide, horns sounding and buses surging forward in clouds of exhaust.

Parking was a nightmare. I finally gave up and pulled into one of the overpriced parking garages, winding up the narrow ramp until I emerged at the very top. Since losing my car in the O'Hare airport garage the year before, I always parked on the top to eliminate the guesswork.

Once we got out things improved. Ruby's mood was contagious and so was the pace of the city. It felt good to be away from South Bend. We went down to the Magnificent Mile and got coffees, then strolled through Macy's and a few smaller stores. At Nordstrom Ruby got serious. She dumped her coffee in the trash and started sifting through racks of clothing like a pro, loading her arms with hangers.

"You weren't kidding. You're going for a whole new look." I eyed the sleek fabrics, mostly in black and neutrals.

She looked up. "Huh? Yeah. Sophisticated."

I browsed for a while myself, but Nordstrom was way beyond my bank account. Ruby went into a dressing room and stayed there; unlike my other friends, she didn't want my opinion. I found myself idling at a makeup counter, trying on thirty-dollar lipsticks. Seriously, who could afford this stuff?

"Stel, I need you to leave and meet me back at the coffee place, okay?" Ruby's voice was urgent, and I whipped around, surprised to see her already done trying on things. "Just go. I'll be there in a few minutes." Her arms were loaded with clothing, and she had an expression that I was starting to recognize: a subtly wired look that meant something was about to go down.

"What are you talking about? I don't want to split up."

"Would you rather get caught shoplifting?" Ruby's whisper froze me solid.

"Oh. Okay," I said in a small voice. "See you there." I don't know why it didn't even occur to me to try to stop her. Maybe because I knew it would be pointless.

I retraced our steps through the mall and down to the coffee shop where we'd started the day. My breath felt funny, almost as if I were the one lifting. The only thing I'd taken in my life was a lipstick from Walgreens when I was ten, and I'd been caught on the way out by security. Mom grounded me for three months. The thought of her face if I was arrested for shoplifting in Nordstrom sent my pulse racing.

For the first time I felt annoyed at Ruby. Shouldn't she have mentioned this part of the plan before sucking me into a trip to Chicago? Then another part of me defended her: at least she'd had the decency to ask me to leave while she did it.

Nordstrom? Was she crazy?

The bell on the door clattered, and Ruby swept into the café, a pile of clothing in her arms. Her hair was windswept and her cheeks rosy. "Can you believe my bag just broke out there?" she confided to the barista. "Do you have another one I could use? Even a garbage bag?"

The barista, a gangly redheaded boy about our age, was only too glad to help. He rummaged under the counter and found a big paper sack with Café Vita printed on the side.

"Thank you so much." Ruby rewarded him with one of her best smiles. She folded the clothes quickly, stacking them into the bag. "Stel? Are you ready? I don't want to be late." Her eyes were glittering with excitement.

I rose to my feet without a word. Ruby gripped my arm and hurried me out the door, plunging into the street as the signal changed. Horns beeped furiously and she laughed, tugging me along.

I was getting madder and madder.

"That was amazing," Ruby crowed. "Heist of the century. Do you know I got a Chanel top that costs five hundred dollars? I tried a new method. I swear you can get away with anything if you act confident enough."

"Congratulations," I snapped.

Ruby looked at me. "What? Oh, come on. Don't get all sanctimonious on me."

"No, it's your business if you want to steal stuff, but you could have told me *before* we drove all the way out here."

"I didn't think you'd care."

"You didn't think I'd care," I repeated. "What if you got caught?"

"I don't get caught."

"Right, that's what every shoplifter says, until they get caught."

"I have a foolproof method," Ruby said smugly. "So chill."

"Fine," I growled.

We walked in silence for a while, and I started to calm down. No one was chasing us. Ruby hadn't gotten caught. And she had tried to protect me. There was no point in staying mad . . . was there?

"What are you going to do next time?" I asked her. "Hold up a bank?"

She grinned, knowing I'd forgiven her. "No, too much

security. Hey, are you hungry? We could get something to eat."

"I can't. I have to get back."

Ruby eyed me curiously. "Your curfew?"

"No, I have to give my brother, Marcus, dinner and get him in bed. My mom is working a double shift."

"How old is your brother?"

"Ten."

"He can't put himself to bed?"

"Not everybody is all grown up by the age of ten, Ruby." I was kidding, but I saw a swift, hurt look pass across her face. "Sorry," I said quickly, not even sure what I was apologizing for.

As we walked to the parking structure, I was still processing the fact that Ruby had ripped off Nordstrom. She was being all charming, asking lots of questions and grinning in this contagious way. I was starting to wonder if she was a sociopath, one of those people with magnetic personalities and absolutely no conscience. It didn't seem out of the realm of possibility.

On the way back to South Bend, I didn't talk much. But Ruby chattered away, still high off her shoplifting spree. She'd taken the Chanel top out of the bag and kept fingering it on her lap.

I felt relieved when I finally dropped her off.

Chapter Five

As usual, Marcus's sneakers were thrown on the porch, caked in mud. Pi, our ancient tomcat, wound around my legs meowing pathetically. Jackie probably forgot to feed him again. I kicked off my shoes and headed into the kitchen. "Jackie? Marcus?"

Nobody answered; but I heard the dim bleeping of a video game, so I knew Marcus was holed up in the den, involved in some simulated pillage and murder.

Then I remembered Jackie was studying with a friend.

Dishes were spilling out of the sink, and the trash needed to go out. The answering machine was blinking: fourteen messages. We're awful about checking messages in my family.

I hit PLAY and scrolled through them quickly: two from Christine, one from Beth, one from Trevor, the rest for Mom or Jackie. Trevor sounded a little pathetic: "Estelle? I miss you.

Um . . . Give me a call." Ruby was right about the hard-to-get thing. Except in this case, I wasn't playing.

I rummaged in the fridge for a carton of yogurt. It was time to go shopping; all we had in there were condiments, Styrofoam containers of ancient takeout, and some withered vegetables, which I always bought out of guilt but nobody ever ate.

The phone seemed to stare at me from its perch on the counter. I was feeling bad about my friends. I'd been so caught up in the excitement of Ruby that I hadn't talked to them much lately. Now I was kind of maxed out on Ruby's craziness, and Beth's gentle voice and calm, polite ways sounded like therapy. I even missed Christine.

I picked up the phone, wishing I could text from our landline because nobody seemed to answer actual phone calls anymore. I tried not to care that we couldn't afford cell phones, but it definitely hurt my social life. Of course, ditching my friends for weeks at a time probably hurt it worse, my conscience whispered. I decided to call everyone right then: Beth, Christine, maybe even Brianna, who was more a soccer friend than anything else.

Beth wasn't around, so I left a message on her voice mail. But Christine answered on the second ring. "Wow, what's the occasion?"

I let the snotty comment slide because she had a point. "Sorry, I know I've been a flake lately. I just wanted to say hi."

"What, Ruby's not around to talk to?"

"I said I was sorry."

"Yeah, well." There was an uncomfortable silence. Then Christine rallied, and we made some small talk. Unfortunately, that's all it was: small talk. Ruby was the proverbial elephant in the room. Or on the phone. Whatever.

Finally I made up an excuse and hung up, feeling totally drained.

It was the first time I realized that my friends weren't just giving me a hard time about Ruby; they were actually mad. Or at least Christine was. I felt guilty but also annoyed. Christine had always been possessive. It was starting to go overboard. Was I not allowed to make new friends?

I decided not to call Brianna after all. The day had already been too much, and what if she was annoyed at me, too? I couldn't handle it at the moment.

It was still an hour until I needed to fix Marcus dinner. I sighed and picked up the sponge: time to tackle the dishes. I turned on the water, but turned it right off again. I thought I heard something—a thump above my head. A couple of seconds later there was another one. That was weird. Jackie was supposed to be at a friend's house studying. Studying . . . right.

I walked to the stairs and climbed quietly, avoiding the creaky spots. My mom's door was cracked open, and laughter spilled into the hall.

"No, you didn't," Jackie said.

"You know I did," said an unmistakable smooth, rich, *male* voice. Was DaShawn Green seriously in our house? DaShawn Green, the überplayer homeboy? DaShawn Green, the pinnacle of hoochie-mama dreams? DaShawn Green the *senior*? I put my eye to the door.

DaShawn was sprawled on my mom's bed, hands tucked behind his head, covers in a bunch at his feet. There was no denying he was gorgeous; but it was spoiled by his clown pants, fake gold chain, and a pair of trainers that probably cost more than a car.

At least he was dressed.

Jackie was standing up, fiddling with the TV on my mom's dresser. She was even more tramped out than usual, with daisy dukes and a ridiculous baby-T that said DADDY'S GIRL—like we even had a dad.

I pushed through the doorway. "What are you guys doing in here?"

DaShawn shot up.

"Oh!" Jackie let out a nervous giggle. "Hey, Stel."

DaShawn relaxed. "Yo, Stella. What's up?"

I pointed at Jackie. "She's thirteen. Did you know that?"

He held up his hands in mock defense. "Don't trip. We're just chillin'."

"Well, last time I checked, half the girls at school were on your jock, so find somebody other than my little sister to *chill* with."

Jackie flushed up to her hair. "Step off, Stella! It's none of your business who my friends are."

DaShawn looked back and forth between us and got off the bed. "You seriously got the wrong idea, but I'm gonna bolt, 'cause it looks like you two got some business to settle. Bye, Shorty. Good seeing you, Stella." DaShawn winked at me— *winked*—and pounded down the stairs and out the front door. As he passed me, I couldn't help noticing a red bandanna peeking out of his pocket.

I turned my wrath on Jackie. "Did he seriously just call you *Shorty*? And what the heck were you doing in here?"

Jackie crossed her arms and slitted her eyes. "DaShawn already told you, chilling."

"Chilling? You mean *screwing*?" I glared at the unmade bed.

Jackie's voice went icy. "You think I'm such a slut, don't you? DaShawn and I are *friends*. Mom has a TV in her room, and I don't. You know she doesn't always make her bed."

"Yeah, like I'm going to believe that. DaShawn is a total player. And what was that red thing in his pocket? Is he fronting like he's a Blood now?"

"He's not fronting anything!" Jackie shouted. "You're so judgmental!" She stalked out and into her own room, slamming the door.

As usual when dealing with Jackie, I was left completely confused. Was I judgmental? And what did she mean by 'He's not fronting anything'? Could he really be in a gang?

I felt a headache coming on, and a flash of resentment at Mom shot through me. I never asked to have a teenage daughter when I was still a teenager myself. This was *her* job.

I went downstairs to take some Advil and get started on Marcus's dinner.

Chapter Six

At Lula's Cafe on Wednesday afternoon, I saw the last person in the world I expected to run into randomly: Mike. He was carrying a coffee in one hand while he tried to pin a couple of fat textbooks to his side with the other arm.

I hurried to help him, because one of the books looked seriously in danger of slipping.

"Thanks!" His face brightened as he recognized me. He set down the books at a table. "Hey, what's up?"

"Not much." I felt embarrassed. That night with him and Sean already seemed like a distant memory, just one in a series of odd adventures that happened with Ruby. Even though Ruby was seeing Sean all the time, she'd never mentioned getting me together with Mike again, so I'd figured he wasn't interested.

"You want to sit down?" He nodded at the empty seat at his

table, a funky old easy chair upholstered in red velvet. Nothing at Lula's matched.

I shrugged. "Let me get my coffee." My stuff was parked on a table close by: my laptop and a giant mocha with lots of whipped cream. I transferred it to his table and sat down.

Mike nodded at my laptop. "You working on school stuff?"

"Yeah. I have an essay due. How about you?"

He rolled his eyes. "Chemistry. I suck at science."

"Really? Usually people who are good at math like science, too."

"Who said I was good at math?"

I took a sip of my drink. "You're a business major, aren't you?"

He grinned. "All that means is I like to sell things. What? Don't look at me like that."

"Like what?" "Like now you think I'm some kind of used car salesman."

I giggled; he'd caught me. I tended to lump all sales types together into one category of slick-talking, not-very-bright con artists, usually with bad hair.

"See? I know what you're thinking. There's such a bias against sales out there. I like people, and I like to negotiate. What's wrong with that?"

"So you're going to Notre Dame to be a salesman?"

"Well, no," Mike admitted. "I'll probably take over my dad's company."

"What's your dad's company?"

He mumbled something.

"What?"

"Long's Drugs."

"What?"

Mike actually blushed. "It's not that big of a deal."

I saw from his discomfort that I should drop it. So he was a rich kid. A *really* rich kid. Being groomed to take over *Long's.* Who knew?

"So what's up with Sean and your friend Ruby?" he asked, changing the subject. "He says she won't call him back."

This was news to me. "I don't know," I said honestly. "Ruby doesn't tell me everything."

"Does she like him?"

"I think so. I mean, you can never really tell with Ruby."

"Yeah, it's driving Sean crazy."

I mentally recorded the conversation. Ruby was going to love hearing this. "Does he take her seriously? Like a real girlfriend? Or does he think she's too young?"

"I think he's really into her. I mean, guys don't talk about this stuff the way you girls do, but I've known him for a long time—we went to high school together—and I've never seen him act this way about a girl." Mike paused. "Besides, I don't think the age difference is such a big deal."

"You don't?"

"No. Three years? That's nothing. Guys *like* to go out with girls a few years younger than them."

Our eyes met, and the air just about crackled.

Mike was looking very handsome. His hair was thick and dirty blond, the kind that would be nice to run your fingers through. He had a little bit of light-colored stubble on his jaw, and it emphasized the difference between him and Trevor, or any of the other guys I'd dated. His sweatshirt fit in that jock way I loved: not too tight, not too loose, but highlighting the firm bulk of his neck, shoulders, and chest. His gaze didn't waver from mine.

"Anyway," he said, breaking the moment, "you going to the game this weekend?"

"What game?"

"Do you live under a rock? The Notre Dame–Boston College game. It's going to be huge."

"I've lived in South Bend my whole life. I don't keep track of every Notre Dame game."

"You're missing out on the best thing about the Bend. Boston College fans are almost as bad as USC. The tailgating alone is going to be epic."

I grinned. "Chugging beer and eating half-cooked hot dogs in the freezing cold? No thanks." Suddenly, I had the thought that he might have been about to invite me. I wished I could swallow my words. Then I remembered Ruby's sermon on playing hard to get and felt a little better.

Mike gave a mock sigh. "You just don't appreciate the finer points of a testosterone frenzy. I'm going to have to school you myself."

I felt a surge of hope.

But he changed the subject, nodding at my computer. "What kind of essay are you working on?"

"History. I'm doing a research project on Fascist Italy."

"Il Duce and all that, huh?"

I nodded, impressed that he knew Mussolini's nickname.

"He was pretty hard-core, but I can see why he appealed to

the peasants," Mike went on. "It's like the Russian Revolution. You get people poor and miserable enough, and they'll take any charismatic guy promising to change things. Are you doing a general history or what?"

"Yeah, pretty much a general history, but I'm finding out a lot about him, too . . ." I was off and running. History was one of my favorite subjects, and it was cool to talk to a guy who seemed to know something about it. I usually kept quiet about that kind of thing in front of guys for fear of looking boring or nerdy.

We talked our way through one refill each, and then I heard Ruby echoing in my head like some kind of guru: "The harder it is to get, the more they want it."

I drained my last sip of mocha and swept my napkins into a ball. "I should probably go now. I have a lot to do today."

"Yeah, me, too." Mike took the cup and napkins from my hand. "I'll throw those away." I packed my laptop into my bag slowly as he cleared the table, hoping he would ask me out, or at least get my phone number. "You drove here? I'll walk you out," he offered.

I was mortified by my beat-up old Mazda, especially now that I knew Mike was the son of—who? the owner? the CEO?—of Long's. But he didn't even seem to notice my car. As I inserted my key in the door, horribly conscious of the lack of automatic locks, he said behind me, "So are you going to give me your number?"

I couldn't help it; I felt a flush spread over my face. "Sure. You got a pen?"

"I'll remember it."

I told him, and he recited it once to himself, then nodded. "Hey, you're wearing a cross. Are you Catholic, too?"

The question came out of nowhere, but it thrilled me. "Yeah," I said, climbing into the front seat.

"Cool." He smiled and shut the door, stepping away from the car.

I drove to the stoplight before I let out a small, excited, very girly whoop.

Chapter Seven

Ruby was thrilled to hear what Sean had said about her to Mike. "It's driving him crazy?" she repeated, radiating satisfaction.

It was Saturday night, and she was camped out on my bed with a bag of mostly puffed-air chips and a huge diet soda. "Nothing tastes better than thin feels" was another mantra that Ruby lived by.

"Yep. 'It's driving Sean crazy.' Those were his exact words."

She grinned up at the ceiling. "Oh, that's good. That is so good."

"Do you like him? Or are you just playing with him?"

"I think I like him. But he was getting bad about calling when he said he would. I hate that."

"A lot of guys do that," I said sagely. "It doesn't mean anything."

"Oh yes, it does. It means they're too confident about you. It means they have the upper hand."

"Maybe they sometimes *forget* to call. Why does everything have to be this power struggle? Like it's a contest, not a relationship?"

Ruby looked at me as if I were incredibly naive. "Because it *is*. Anyway, he's not doing that anymore."

"Now he's calling you all the time because you stopped calling him back?" I guessed.

She nodded. "Utterly predictable. But whatever. I met somebody else interesting, an English grad student. He's smart as hell."

"But I thought you just said maybe you like Sean."

"Maybe I do. That doesn't mean I'm committed to him. This is such a misogynist culture. It's ridiculous: you go out with a guy one time, and he's like a dog peeing on his territory. You're not allowed to talk to anybody else."

"But if you like him, don't you want him to be like that?" I had grown up thinking that the ultimate goal was to get a guy you liked to finally commit. I couldn't wrap my head around Ruby's attitude.

"No! Come on, Stel, think about it. It's so degrading to think you have to catch a man."

I didn't say it, but as far as I could tell, that was about all Ruby spent her time doing: catching men.

I must have looked doubtful, because she said, "Attracting them, keeping them interested—that's part of the game. But giving exclusive rights to some guy who took you out for pizza? Or hooked up with you at a party? That is so weak. It's totally limiting you during the best years of your life. Back in the old days they had to give you, like, horses and money and jewelry; and they couldn't even kiss you unless they were going to marry you. *That's* value."

I raised my eyebrows. Ruby was good at putting a new spin on things. The way I'd been taught, women were crazy-oppressed until about 1920, when we got the right to vote; and things had been getting slowly better ever since.

"Anyway, he's taking me for granted. He needs a little competition. This new guy? James? He's doing his dissertation on Chekhov, but I swear he looks like he could kill a wolf with his bare hands," Ruby said.

"You like that?" I asked.

"You don't?" she asked back.

We looked at each other and giggled. Ruby was so nuts; there was never a boring second with her.

Ruby sat up and changed the subject abruptly. "I got you an ID."

"What?"

"Yeah. Here, hold on a second." She swung her legs over the side of the bed and scooped up her purse, digging through tubes of lip gloss and about a year's worth of wadded-up receipts. She pulled out a little rectangle of plastic and read aloud, "Anna Marie Lopez."

I grabbed it from her. It was a real Illinois ID. I looked at the year. "This says I'm supposed to be . . ."

"Twenty-six."

I stared at the picture on the front, then burst out laughing. "Are you kidding? She doesn't even look like me!"

Ruby took the ID back, frowning. "Yes, she does. Look,

brown hair, brown eyes, five six, one fifteen. That's you."

"No, it's not! Look at her hair! And her nose!"

"Hair changes, and the nose isn't that bad. Well, it's a little pointy. But maybe they'll think it's a bad camera angle."

"They?"

"Bouncers, cashiers, whoever."

I flopped on my bed and closed my eyes. "Ruby, I am not going to try to use that pathetic excuse for an ID. Anna Marie looks like a crackhead. I would be offended if anyone believed it was me. Where did you get it, anyway?"

"Pinnacle Athletic Club. They get IDs all the time from visitors. They keep them at the front desk. I made friends with one of the trainers."

"Another guy for your harem?"

"No. He's just a friend." Ruby wrinkled her nose. "He's short."

There was the sound of the front door and the familiar creaks and thuds as Mom came into the house, dropped her bag, and pried off her work shoes.

Ruby bounded out of bed and downstairs, with me at her heels. "Hi, Mrs. Chavez."

"Hi there, Ruby."

Ruby was always eager to see my mom; in fact, I'd never seen her so perky and talkative with any other adult.

Mom, for her part, was warming up to Ruby. She still thought Ruby was smooth, I could tell; but it was hard not to be won over when Ruby turned on the charm full blast.

"How was your day, Mrs. Chavez?"

"Fine, hon. Thanks for asking. Is Marcus home yet? The Connors were supposed to drop him off after swim practice."

Mom looked worn-out, as usual. Her uniform had a fresh stain down the front, and I noticed that it was hanging a little loosely around her shoulders. Lots of moms got plumper as they got older, but mine seemed to be shrinking away into nothing.

"No, he hasn't gotten home yet. You want me to make you a sandwich? I think there are some cold cuts in the fridge," I offered.

Mom sank onto our old corduroy couch and stuck her feet on the coffee table, nudging aside a couple of Jackie's schoolbooks. "Yeah, that would be really nice."

"I'll help." Ruby hurried to the kitchen, fishing through cupboards and drawers until she found a plate and knife. I handed her the meat and bread and mayo, and watched as she made a perfect sandwich, trimming the edges and slicing it in a neat diagonal. Most friends put up with parents as a necessary intrusion, but it might have been a toss-up if Ruby would rather hang out with my mom or me, if she had to pick.

"Thanks, Ruby," Mom said, accepting the sandwich Ruby handed her. "Stella, any chance you have time to do a shopping run? We're low on everything, and I have another shift tonight."

"Sure," I said.

"I can help you," Ruby offered.

Mom smiled at Ruby and said, "You're a sweetie."

Ruby practically glowed. I felt kind of bad for her. It was so obvious she was soaking up Mom because Gina was such a slouch in the mothering department. When Gina was around, which wasn't that often, she wafted around the house like a gorgeous ghost, sipping coffee, reading academic journals— she was a researcher in the bio lab at Notre Dame—and talking on the phone. She barely acknowledged Ruby and me except to say hi and ask a few basic questions about our day. I was desperately curious to know more about her, and other things, too, like what happened to Ruby's dad. But I knew not to bring it up. I could feel a ten-foot wall around *that* subject.

Besides, I hadn't told her about *my* dad, either. I guess there were some things both of us were keeping private.

We hung around at my house for a while watching TV and then finally headed out to do the shopping. I'd been in charge of groceries for years, and I wheeled through Frank's quickly, filling the cart with staples. Ruby followed me, taking random things off the shelves and stealing candy from the bins like a kid. Then we turned the corner to the produce section . . . and she completely stopped.

At the other end of the section, standing in front of a big fruit display, were Sean and a girl. The girl was definitely college age and cute, in a wholesome sort of way. Her face was sprinkled with freckles, and her hair was a ripple of the prettiest strawberry blond. They were talking animatedly, and then the girl took a step closer to Sean and tapped him on the arm with an apple like she was giving him a mock-spank for something he'd said.

Ruby yanked me back behind the aisle. "Come on. Let's get out of here."

"What? Don't you want to say hi? . . ." I trailed off as I took in her flush and the furious look in her eyes.

"He's obviously busy," Ruby snarled.

"That's probably just somebody he knows from school. Watch, when we go over there, he'll introduce you as his girlfriend."

Ruby glared at me and whirled around, then took off running out of the store. I thought about taking what we'd already gotten through the checkout; but considering the look on Ruby's face, I figured I'd better not take any chances.

Irrational or not, Ruby was freaking out, and I needed to be there for her.

I left the cart and went to find her in the parking lot. It's a good thing I did, because she was heading away from my car, head down, jogging toward the street. I had to run fast to catch up.

"Ruby!"

She lifted her head, and I was astounded to see that her eyes were bright with tears.

"Come on! I'll take you home."

Wordlessly, she turned around and followed me to the car. It was only when we pulled out of the lot that she let the tears out in big, shuddering sobs, burying her face in her hands. Her thin shoulders shook.

After a minute I said helplessly, "It's okay. She's probably just a friend"; but Ruby gave me such an evil glare that I shut up.

By the time we turned onto her street a few minutes later, Ruby wasn't crying anymore. I idled in front of her house, not sure what to say. Finally she asked huskily, "Do you want to come in?"

"Do you want me to?"

"Yes." She sniffed, staring out the window as I parked. "You probably think I'm crazy."

"Not at all," I lied.

When we got inside, Ruby flicked on the lights and

turned up the thermostat. As usual, Gina was gone. Normally we'd go straight to Ruby's room and stay there, but today Ruby went into the dining room. The table had been wearing the same perfect settings since they'd moved in. She leaned over and opened a large, carved-wood cabinet. Inside was a line of bottles and upside-down glasses. Ruby tucked a bottle of Absolut under her arm and headed to her room.

We settled into our regular spots: Ruby nestled in the mound of blankets on her bed and me on the beanbag chair. I watched her warily. I wasn't sure she was in any condition to handle the vodka. She unscrewed the top and took two long gulps, lowering the bottle with no expression.

"Are you okay?" I ventured.

"Yeah, I'm fine." Ruby took another drink and let out a heavy sigh. "Did you think she was pretty?"

"Not really. I mean, she looked kind of normal, you know?" Seeing Ruby's expression, I added, "Like some kind of farm girl. A little hickish. Not Sean's type at all. I can't believe you're even worried about her. I'm sure they're just friends from school or something."

"Right," Ruby said darkly. "Did you see how they were laughing?"

"Friends laugh." I wanted to shake her by the shoulders, bring her back to reality.

"If they were friends, how come I don't know about her?"

"Do you know about every person Sean has classes with? Of course not. They probably just ran into each other."

"No, it looked like they were together. There was only one cart."

"Not everybody shops with a cart, you know. Maybe

she only had to pick up milk or something."

"Then what was she doing in the produce aisle?"

I could tell there was no arguing with Ruby. I tried another tactic. "Well, aren't you seeing other people, anyway? That guy? The English major?"

"He was nothing. We just went out a couple times. I never even kissed him." Ruby stared gloomily out the window. I couldn't believe how hypocritical she was being, but it wasn't the time to point it out.

"Ruby, you have nothing to worry about. Sean is head over heels for you. It's so obvious. He'll probably call in, like, ten minutes, and you'll realize this whole thing is ridiculous."

"If he calls I won't pick up."

"What?"

"I'm done. I can't trust him." Ruby took another sip of vodka. "Once I can't trust someone, I'm through."

"But he didn't do anything wrong! You just saw him laughing with some girl in the grocery store. They could have been, like, lab partners or something."

"I don't care. I'm done."

I saw by Ruby's face that she was serious.

I felt a shiver of worry. It's a strange moment when you realize someone you care about is a little . . . off. I felt suddenly protective. "You want to watch a movie? Let's break out your mom's chocolates and buy some juice or something for the vodka. We can rent a crazy eighties movie."

Ruby perked up. "Yeah, we should order pizza, too. Can we order pizza?"

"Yeah!" I agreed a little too heartily. To be honest, Ruby ordering a pizza worried me more than the drinking. She lived on salads and sushi-to-go and complained if she gained even half an ounce.

"Sausage and mushrooms," said Ruby, closing her eyes as she took another swig. "With extra cheese."

I made it all happen. I ordered the pizza, rented the movie, did a 7-Eleven run to pick up cranberry juice for the vodka. I hauled some blankets to the living room, and we got comfortable on the couch.

We watched Corey Feldman and Corey Haim slaughter ridiculous vampires in *The Lost Boys* as Ruby finished off three cranberry vodkas, four slices of pizza dripping with cheese, and a couple of her mom's truffles. Her cell phone rang several times, but she acted as if it wasn't there. Before the movie ended, Ruby sank into a drunkish doze. Her cell phone buzzed again, and I glanced at the screen before turning it off. Sean.

Feeling sad, I tiptoed out of her living room to get my keys. I'd only had two weak drinks, and they'd pretty much worn off. It was time for me to go food shopping.

Chapter Eight

My friends cornered me the next day at school. It was interesting timing, considering they couldn't have known about what had happened the night before—but Christine always did have a radar for those kinds of things.

I was on the way to precalc, and Christine bumped my shoulder and said, "Hey, have you seen my friend Stella? She hasn't been around much lately."

I smiled. "You are so funny."

Beth linked arms with me and said, "Hey, lady. Just to warn you, Hollins gave us a sick pop quiz first period."

"Thanks." I grimaced. Precalc and I had an uneasy truce based on hours of studying. But a pop quiz could always throw me off.

We chatted about random stuff for a few minutes, but when I came to the turnoff for my classroom, Christine said out of the blue, "Stella, is everything cool?"

I looked at her, confused. That was a weird question, and a strange place to ask it. "What are you talking about?"

She and Beth moved closer, until we were in a tight knot in the hall. Christine looked at me steadily. "You're just acting different since you started hanging out with Ruby."

"She seems kind of wild," Beth said. "Don't you think?"

I was floored. "Yeah—I mean, she's a little wild; but she's a good person."

"That's good," Beth said uncertainly.

"Okay," said Christine. "We just wanted to ask."

I scowled. I knew they cared about me, but this felt like nosiness. "Well, thanks, I guess. I'll see you guys later," I said coolly. And I walked into precalc.

But that wasn't the end of it. A few hours later I got more chaff from Coach Turner, who was flaming mad that I missed one lousy practice to take Ruby home on Friday when she wasn't feeling well. Coach stared at me with her piercing blue eyes and her arms folded across her chest and asked, "Stella, how important is soccer to you?"

What was I supposed to say to *that*?

"Very?" I answered.

Coach nodded. "That's what I thought. So please don't let me hear again that you missed practice to play chauffeur."

Even after a couple of sweaty hours doing a scrimmage, I went home in a bad mood. It was as if the universe was telling me to question my friendship with Ruby.

I wasn't making a mistake—was I? Yes, she was wild. But she was also fun. And smart. And brave. And loyal.

And a lot more interesting than most other things in my life at the moment.

✳

I got a call from Mike that night. It wasn't exactly the call I'd fantasized about. He cut right in: "Stella? Is Ruby okay? She's not calling Sean back, and he's kind of worried."

"Um, she's fine. Maybe she's just busy."

"When did you last see her? Sean thinks something might have happened to her. They usually talk every night."

"She was at school today." I began shuffling papers on the counter, fidgeting even though he couldn't see me.

I wanted to bluff for Ruby; but Mike wasn't dumb, and I knew Sean wasn't, either. Eventually they'd figure out she was blowing Sean off, and then I'd have to answer some questions.

There was a muffled sound, and I heard Mike say, "She was in school today." I couldn't help but smile. They were grown-up college men, but this felt so high school. Then Mike was back on the phone. "Would you tell her to call Sean? Tell her he's worried, okay?"

"Sure."

Obviously relieved to be done with that, Mike turned the conversation to other things, asking about my day and bringing up some new points about the history stuff we'd talked about at Lula's. Mike was sharp, and he knew a lot of facts; but I found that I could keep up with him.

When we were finally about to get off the phone half an hour later, he said, almost as an afterthought, "What are you doing for dinner on Friday?"

"Nothing," I said.

"Do you like Chinese?"

A grin broke out on my face. "Yes." We made plans for him to pick me up at seven.

When I hung up the phone, I was so excited I couldn't stop smiling. It wasn't normal for me to be this giddy about a guy, and I loved it.

Afterward, I called Ruby to let her know Sean was asking about her.

"I don't want to talk about him." She sounded distant. "It's over."

If Christine or Beth were acting this crazy, I'd totally call her on it. But I didn't bother, with Ruby. Somehow I knew it wouldn't do any good. Carefully, I asked, "What do you want me to tell Mike?"

She sighed loudly into the phone as if it were a chore to come up with an excuse. "Tell him I'm seeing someone else."

I couldn't help myself. "Ruby! That's mean!" I blurted out.

"Well, tell him whatever you want, then." Her voice was flat and cold.

Clearly, the conversation was closed. "Whatever," I said, and hung up annoyed.

As usual, I was the one left holding the bag. What was I supposed to tell Mike? This could make things weird between us. Maybe he'd decide high school girls were immature after all.

My friends' comments from earlier came back to me. Ruby *was* wild—and there was something off about the way she related to guys. It worried me.

I was on edge about Ruby, and Mike, too, until Friday, when Mike picked me up for our date. Mom was working, and Marcus was spending the night at his friend Liam's; but Jackie was home, sacked out on the couch flicking through channels.

I was not thrilled about Jackie meeting Mike. For one, I didn't want him noticing her long, tanned legs kicked up over the back of our couch; and secondly, her tongue had a tendency to flap. She was sure to broadcast to Mom in the most alarming way possible that Mike looked older than your average high school guy.

At six-thirty I started watching out the window, hoping I'd see Mike pull up so I could run outside. Of course, the one moment I was in the bathroom, he knocked on the door. I ran, but Jackie got there first. She was just opening it when I came up behind her. Mike looked handsome and clean-cut in a dark blue pullover and jeans, his face freshly shaved. I saw him through Jackie's eyes and felt a twinge of pride.

"You're Mike?" Jackie asked incredulously.

He grinned. "Yep. And you must be Jackie."

I grabbed my purse off the hook and said, "Bye, Jackie. I'll be home in a couple hours."

"Where should I tell Mom you went?" Now, that was pure Jackie nosiness. We both knew Mom wouldn't be home till late. I glared at her and shut the door. Every mention of Mom was a strike against Mike taking me seriously.

Mike chuckled. "Are you embarrassed?"

"Yeah," I admitted as he let me into the car.

"Don't be. I know you're almost eighteen, and I'm fine with it, okay? I just got out of high school a year and a half ago."

I gave him a grateful look.

From there the night kept getting better. The Chinese place wasn't very good, but that just gave us a lot to laugh about: the dragon decor, scarily bright-pink sweet and sour chicken, and old-school place mats printed with the Chinese zodiac. Mike told me he knew how to do origami and butchered a whole stack of napkins by folding them into funny shapes and naming them things like Lucky Snake and Mating Crane. He had the best hands: strong and large, with little gold hairs on the back. So manly. I don't know why, but I felt like hands could tell you a lot about a person.

The only awkward moment was when Mike asked why Ruby still wasn't calling Sean. I hesitated but then just told him the truth. Ruby was done with Sean, anyway, so why would it matter?

Mike looked puzzled. "That is so strange. Sean isn't seeing anybody else. I mean, I don't know any redheads that he's friends with, but it was probably someone from one of his classes."

"That's what I told her," I said.

After that we moved on to other topics, and finally Mike drove me home close to ten. We were quiet as we drove, just listening to music; but there was a subtle tension building in the car.

The good kind.

When Mike pulled up at my house, he cut the motor and we sat in the dark, looking at each other. I felt excited yet oddly comfortable. Mike's eyes were intense. He twined his fingers through mine, and I thrilled at how his hands completely encompassed mine.

"Thanks for coming out with me," he whispered.

His lips brushed my cheek very gently, and then my other cheek, and finally my mouth. Our mouths molded perfectly, and I realized with a quick throb of excitement that we kissed well together, matched each other. I lost myself in the kiss.

After a few moments he pulled back and stroked my face. "Can I call you tomorrow?"

"Of course, silly." We both laughed a little.

I got out of the car, ecstatic and heady, and he watched me up the steps. When I walked in, I was practically floating.

"You hooked up with him," Jackie accused. She was sitting there waiting for me.

"What are you doing still awake?"

"It's not even ten! It's Friday!"

"Oh." I gave her a silly grin and headed upstairs toward my room.

"Stella! You hooked up with him!" she called.

"I have no idea what you're talking about." I wasn't fooling anyone, but I didn't care.

Chapter Nine

Over the next month Ruby and I settled into a pretty regular best-friend schedule of lunches together, rides home after school, and long afternoons talking. Ruby *was* my best friend now, no question, and everyone knew it.

It was a transition I needed to make. I had been friends with Beth and Christine since elementary school, and I loved them; but I felt kind of stuck in my identity when I was with them.

With Ruby I was someone new, someone with more spice.

Ruby's confidence was contagious. I know it sounds stupid, but after a few months of her calling me "hot Latin lover" and "sexy Latina," I started to see my curvy hips and rear as a good thing. I started thinking maybe my skin *was* beautiful, like she said, instead of too dark. And I liked that Ruby didn't know my entire history. She was getting to know me for who I was becoming, not who I used to be.

I actually thought I was balancing things pretty well,

catching up with Christine and Brianna after soccer practices, going for coffee with Beth on the weekends, and talking on the phone with everybody at least once a week. But it was still way different from how it used to be.

I should have known Christine wouldn't take it without a fight. She was stone loyal and possessive, and she hated change.

I immediately knew something was up when Christine, Beth, and Brianna met me coming out of chemistry one afternoon. It was the slightly wired look on Christine's face, the anxious one on Beth's face, and the fact that all three of them were together when normally it would just be Christine and Beth.

"What?" I said.

"We just need to talk to you," Christine said. "Is that okay?"

What could I say?

I followed them to our favorite table in the quad, which was recessed behind the library and somewhat private. Beth squeezed my hand as we sat down.

"We're worried about you," Christine started.

"And Ruby," added Brianna.

I frowned at her. She didn't belong there. Brianna was a fringe friend, more of a teammate than anything else; this wasn't her business. Christine probably invited her for more effect.

Christine leaned forward, keeping her voice down. "People are saying stuff. Like Ruby and you do all these drugs, and you're hooking up with college guys and being a slut."

"I don't care what people say," I said with as much dignity as I could. But I did care.

"We miss you," said Beth.

"And we're worried you're changing. You keep missing soccer practice because of her," added Christine.

"That was once because she was sick and needed a ride home."

"Twice. Coach was mad," said Brianna.

"Everybody says she does a lot of drugs," Beth said timidly. "You wouldn't get into that stuff, would you?"

"No! How long have you guys known me? And I've never seen Ruby do anything except smoke a little weed, which I could say for all of you except Beth."

"Well, what about the thing with the guys?" Christine said. "Everybody's talking about it. Trevor is mad that you're putting out for all these Notre Dame guys after you said you were a virgin."

"I'm still a virgin!" I roared. "Not that it's any of your business!"

Beth's mouth trembled, and I wished I could reel my words back in. "I mean, it is your business. You're my friends, but I feel like you're ganging up on me right now. You've known me forever. Do you really think I'd do that stuff?"

"What are we supposed to think? You don't eat with us anymore, and you barely talk to us, except for like these pity calls. You never hang out, and you don't tell us anything you do." Christine's eyes gleamed with hurt and anger.

"Elsa's gone, and now it feels like we're losing you," Beth added.

"And I don't care what you say," said Christine. "Ruby is a slut. You can tell just by looking at her."

"Totally," said Brianna. She almost sounded as if she were enjoying herself.

I ignored Brianna and turned to Beth and Christine. "I'm sorry if you guys feel like I'm picking Ruby over you. I'm . . . we've been doing the same thing for ten years. I guess I'm ready for a change. It doesn't mean I don't love you guys."

It was the wrong thing to say.

"I really don't care who you hang out with," Christine said coldly. "I was trying to look out for you by telling you what everybody is saying. It's obvious you already made your choice, so why don't you cut the pity party and just hang out with her full-time?"

"Yeah," said Brianna.

Beth sniffed.

"Is that what you want?" I asked. I could feel the tears boiling behind my eyes, and I took a breath to steady myself. I am *not* a person who breaks down.

"Yes," Christine said defiantly.

Brianna nodded.

"Beth?" I asked in a half whisper.

"I feel like you're hanging out with us just to be nice. I don't want that," she said quietly.

"I'm not!" My voice cracked. "How can you think that? We've been friends since kindergarten! Doesn't that count for something?"

Tears began to stream down Beth's cheeks.

"I don't know. Does it?" Christine spat out. "Come on," she said, putting a protective arm around Beth. And they got up and walked away.

Chapter Ten

I didn't tell Ruby what happened with my friends. I was afraid she would minimize it and say they were just petty idiots and I should forget about them. She wouldn't understand that it really mattered, losing them. It shook me to my core.

But I wasn't going to let anybody tell me who I was allowed to be friends with. So I shut it out, completely blocked them from my mind.

I had plenty of practice not thinking about things that hurt, anyway. Like my dad. I still hadn't told Ruby why he left. Some things are just too painful to even say out loud.

Ruby had some things she didn't talk about, too. She never said a word about Gina or *her* missing dad. She did talk a lot about guys, though: past guys, present guys, whoever. She was like part shrink, part soldier, making plans to keep them in line.

After the Sean debacle, it took Ruby about a week to get a

whole new herd of guys. I couldn't figure out how she picked them up so quickly: it had to be pheromones or something. There was a James Dean–looking guy who cleaned the floors at IUSB, a gorgeous dreadlocked Notre Dame student from Trinidad, a sleazy grunge rocker who worked at the Texaco and had to be at least twenty-five. . . . Ruby didn't care.

She was collecting men like stamps.

By then we had developed a weekly outing to The South Bend Chocolate Company, home of everything delicious and fattening. Ruby said they had the only decent espresso in town. And they had a chocolate dessert I loved called El Diablo that really was the devil. Tuesday was our locked-in date.

We sat outside even though it was freezing because Ruby wanted to smoke. She was clutching a giant Americano and chain-smoking, and I was working on an El Diablo the size of my head. We were hashing over whether or not it would be fun to go to prom. Ruby, of course, was against it, but I felt that it was a life landmark that shouldn't be missed.

"It's so high school," Ruby said, flicking ashes. "I mean, they have punch and chaperones. What kind of party is that?"

"It's tradition! It's what every girl looks forward to from seventh grade on!"

"What? Buying a cheap bridesmaid dress, getting wasted on forties, and hooking up with a horny seventeen-year-old in the back of some rented limo?"

"Has anyone ever told you that you're stuck up?"

But Ruby was distracted.

I followed her eyes to the door, which was swinging open to let another customer into the courtyard. He was tall and lean and at least forty, maybe even older, with short salt-and-pepper hair. He was wearing jeans and a fitted, long-sleeved black T-shirt, carrying a leather folder in one hand and a drink in the other. He filled out his T-shirt too perfectly for it to be an accident; each muscle under there had to be the result of hours in the gym. And the shirt looked designer, like Calvin Klein or something.

Ruby's eyes flickered over him appreciatively as he walked past us to another table. "Silver fox," she murmured.

He was handsome, no doubt. He had strong, masculine features, sculpted lips, and sharp, dark eyes. He met my glance and smiled ever so slightly. I blushed and looked down. Ruby studied him openly for a few moments, blowing smoke rings with a half smile. Then we got caught up in our conversation again.

Fifteen minutes passed, maybe twenty, and then the man rose and tossed his cup in the trash. Instead of heading for the sidewalk, he walked over to us. "This is yours if you put out that cigarette." His voice was amused, as if he'd made some private joke. He set a hundred-dollar bill on the table in front of Ruby.

She gaped. "What?"

"That's yours if you put out the cigarette," he repeated.

Ruby's eyebrows flew up. It was the first time I'd seen her completely caught off guard. Then she tilted back her head and laughed, and stubbed her cigarette out in the ashtray. "That's a pretty good deal for me."

"It is," the man agreed. "And if I see you here again not smoking, I'll give you another just like it." He turned and walked away.

Ruby picked up the bill and examined it. "Can you believe that? He just gave me a hundred dollars!" Her voice was squeaky.

"Are you sure it's real?"

"Yeah, it's real; look at it! He must be loaded! That was crazy! What should I do?"

"I don't know, put it in your bank account or something. Buy a new outfit."

"That's not what I mean! Did you hear what he said? If he sees me not smoking here again, he'll give me more!"

"Well, that's kind of vague. I mean, you can't stake out the place or something. Who knows when he'll come back?"

Ruby raised her eyebrows and looked at me. I knew that look, and I grinned. It was good to see her excited. Despite all the new guys, she'd been flat since Sean. "You *are* going to stake out the place," I guessed.

"Hell, yes. Wouldn't you? Did you see how hot he was?"

"Yeah, and like forty."

"So? Maybe he's thirty and just prematurely gray."

"Thirty is still old!"

Ruby gave me a withering look. We'd had this conversation before, because Ruby was always scandalizing me with her grad students. "Stella, you're in this cultural bubble, okay? For thousands of years, older guys have been with younger women. In other countries they still do it."

"And women are drawn to the best providers; and men are drawn to fertility and beauty, so older men and younger women are a perfect match," I finished in a singsong voice.

"Well, at least you've been listening."

I changed tracks. "Do you think he's some kind of health freak? Like a no-smoking extremist?"

"Maybe. Or maybe he's just an eccentric millionaire. A philanthropist." Ruby's brow furrowed. "Do I look, like, poor?"

I had to laugh. Even post-Sean, Ruby was still looking very classy. The liquid liner had disappeared, the lip gloss was paler, and her roots had been covered up with a trip to the salon. "The exact opposite, actually."

"Well, I say we come back every day until we see him again."

"We? I have soccer practice three nights a week, and Coach has been freaking out on me. Anyway, are you going to give me half your profits?"

"Are you kidding? Of course not."

"I didn't think so."

We grinned at each other. I was at peace with Ruby's general selfishness. There was no malice behind it. And besides, her loyalty and charisma more than made up for it.

While Ruby would chew men up and spit them out in shreds, I knew in my gut that she was my friend for life.

Ruby staked out South Bend Chocolate Company all week, filling me in on the phone each night. It wasn't that easy to pull off without a car. I could only give her rides a couple times a week, and I drew the line at picking her up at night. She finally convinced Jackson, the Texaco worker, to give her rides home on his motorcycle.

The whole thing was ridiculous, but I still hoped the guy would show up again, if only to keep her distracted from Sean.

Then, a week later, when we were out on our coffee-dessert ritual, freezing our tails off and conspicuously not smoking, Ruby gave a squeal and hissed, "Don't look."

It was torture not to turn around, but a moment later he was in front of us, smiling a half smile. This time he was in jeans and a gray sweater that picked up the glints of silver in his hair.

"It appears you're not smoking," he commented, never taking his eyes off Ruby. I couldn't blame him for staring at her, but it bugged me that he acted as if I didn't exist.

"Someone convinced me to kick the habit," she said in a faintly mocking tone.

"Really?" The man bent toward her and lifted the corner of her scarf to his face, breathing in. There was something so sensual about the way he did it that I felt embarrassed and a little shocked. "It doesn't smell like you've quit. Still, I'm glad you're not smoking right now." He tossed another hundred-dollar bill on the table and walked away.

It was the second time I'd seen Ruby at a complete loss, and both times were because of this man. She stared after him googly-eyed. "That was so hot," she breathed.

"Next time you're buying," I told her.

"I'll take you to Trio's if this keeps up. You know what? I was an idiot for staking the place out all week. He came back on the same day at the same time. He wanted to see me."

"He caught you. He knows you're still smoking."

"Yeah, he's sharp," Ruby agreed.

"I think this is some kind of elaborate seduction."

"I hope so," she said fervently. "I really hope so."

Chapter Eleven

The following week Ruby tactfully disinvited me to the coffee shop. "I think the guy wants to talk to me, Stel, and he might not really want to do it when you're around."

"He doesn't strike me as the shy type."

"You know what I mean."

I just looked at her. I *did* know what she meant, but I was a little ticked off at her for getting all that money and now bailing on me to go after some hot but ridiculously too-old guy.

"Stel, please don't be mad? This one week I'm going alone, but after that it will be back to normal. I just want to give him a chance to hit on me."

"Whatever," I said.

And that was that. Ruby went alone, and I made plans with Mike, who had been morphing into a real boyfriend. We hadn't had any kind of "talk," but we both kind of knew we weren't seeing anybody else. The plans on this particular day were a big, hairy deal, and I was so nervous I was sweating.

Mike was meeting my mom.

Let me say that I was not the one who instigated it. This was all Mike. In fact, I was very much against it. But he kept insisting, and we had reached that awkward point where if I said no one more time, he'd think I was embarrassed of him or didn't like him enough or something.

There was a lot of irony in that. I *was* embarrassed, but not of him. It was the waitress, messy house thing again. Mike was brilliant. He went to one of the best schools in the country. His dad was the owner of Long's. I was afraid he would walk into my house and meet my mom and have a vision of me in twenty-five years: a little unkempt, with food stains on my shirt, and not much of a housekeeper.

Then I'd get mad at myself for even thinking that way. Mom was an angel who worked her fingers off for us, solid to the core, loving and stable and all things good. If Mike couldn't see that, then I didn't want to be with him.

At least that's what I told myself.

But it wasn't just that. Mom had been single since my dad left, never bringing home strange men or going on dates like other single moms. She said she'd seen too many of her friends bring the wrong guy around their kids, and she didn't want anybody complicating the picture until we were grown.

Mom and I were a team, always working hard, backing each other up. I had this weird feeling that I was betraying her by getting serious with a boy. When I got married or moved out to go to college, it would be like Dad leaving her all over again.

Crazy, I know. Still, the afternoon Mike was coming over,

I was fidgety and snappy to the point where Mom put her hands on my shoulders, looked me in the eyes, and said, "Estelle, will you please relax? You're driving me nuts."

"I'm *fine*. Do you know where the duster is?"

Mom gave a sigh of frustration. "I don't know! Do we even have a duster anymore? I thought Pi ate the feathers off the old one." Our cat had the digestive system of a garbage disposal.

I glared at her. "That's the problem with this house! When things break, we don't replace them! Everything is a mess!"

"Stella, cut it out!"

And at that lovely moment the doorbell rang.

Mom ruffled my hair and whispered, "Calm down; I know you're just nervous. It will be fine." Then she answered the door. Mike, to my embarrassment, had a bouquet of calla lilies for me and a pink bakery box of cookies for my mom.

She beamed as she peeked under the lid. "Almond horns and Russian tea cakes! Did Stella tell you my favorites?"

"No, but they're my favorites, too," Mike told her, earning like a hundred brownie points.

"Well, let me get a plate and some milk, and we can have some right now. And I'll cut the stems on these and get them in some water. Go on, you two sit down, and I'll be right out." Mom bustled away to the kitchen, then popped her head out and said with a smile, "By the way, it's very nice to meet you."

Mike grinned at me and took a seat on our couch. I sat stiffly next to him, trying to cover the rip in the faded upholstery. He put his hand over mine. "You have a good day?"

"Pretty good. Normal."

"You heard from Ruby yet about the perv?" I had told Mike all about the man, and he was convinced the guy was a dirty old pervert trying to get Ruby psychologically hooked. He couldn't believe she was meeting him alone.

"No," I told him. "They're probably meeting right now. I'll tell you the second I hear anything."

Then Mom came back out, carrying a stack of plates and paper napkins. I cringed when she handed Mike the plate with the chip, but he didn't seem to notice.

"So, Mike, you're studying business at Notre Dame?" Mom asked. At first she had flipped out about Mike being in college; but she calmed down when she realized he was nineteen, only two years older than me.

"Yeah. I'm still doing my core classes, though, like English comp and my science, history, and religion credits."

"Stella mentioned you're Catholic. Do you go to the Basilica of the Sacred Heart?"

I stared at my feet. Leave it to Mom to bring up religion in the first thirty seconds.

"Actually, I go to mass in the chapel in my residence hall. It's smaller, but it's nice because it's right downstairs from my room. Where do you guys go to church?"

"We go to St. Lucille's. It's wonderful." And Mom was off, gushing about Father Garcia, our priest, and the community outreach our parish did, and the renovation of the Chapel of St. Mary.

Mike, always a good conversationalist, kept drawing her out, asking more questions; and after a while I started to get the funny feeling that he was actually enjoying himself. They had gotten into Vatican II, and it was over my head; but they both seemed to know what they were talking about. It occurred to me that they had found the one topic where Mom came off as pretty educated. I felt a burst of gratitude toward God; I had certainly sent Him enough desperate prayers about this meeting.

Then the phone rang; and when I excused myself, I swear they hardly noticed I was leaving.

It was Ruby. "Stella, you're not going to believe this. So I was sitting there, and he, I mean, *Kenneth*—" She was babbling and completely hyped. I had to cut her off.

"Ruby, Mike's over right now meeting my mom. I can't really talk. Can I call you later?"

"Can you just come over? You are so not going to believe what happened."

"Okay, I'll come over when Mike leaves. You're going to be home?"

"Yes! Hurry!"

I hung up the phone and went back to the living room. Mom glanced up. "It wasn't for me, was it?"

"No, it was Ruby."

Mike raised his eyebrows and mouthed, "Perv?"

I shrugged. I was dying to find out myself.

Then it was back to church talk, and somehow Mom worked in an invitation for Mike to come to St. Lucille's with us sometime, if he wanted to see it.

"I would love to," he told her, looking delighted.

His visit stretched into nearly an hour, despite Mom's quickly approaching shift. I'd planned it that way so things couldn't go too long; but now it seemed as if my worries had been pointless. Mike and Mom just plain clicked. I felt guilty that I'd been afraid of them meeting.

When it was time for Mike to leave, Mom gave him a kiss

on the cheek. I walked him out to his car and stood hugging my chest against the cold, beaming.

He was beaming, too. "That went really well, huh?"

"Yeah. She loves you."

"I was a little nervous," he confessed. "I thought she'd think I was too old for you or something."

"Two years isn't that big of a deal."

"She's such a sweetheart. She's so momish. Nothing like my mom."

"What's your mom like?"

"Um . . . polished." Mike changed the subject. "You going to call Ruby now?"

"Actually, I'm going over there. She's freaking out, but in a good way, I think. She told me to come over as soon as you left."

"Well, call me and let me know what happened."

"I will." I laughed. "Just for the record, whoever said guys don't like to gossip clearly hasn't met you."

"So?" Then Mike leaned down, and I stretched up, and we had an awkward, sweet kiss. Our kisses still felt new. "Call me later," he said.

"I will." I waved as he drove away and then sprinted inside to grab my keys.

Mom was sitting on the couch eating cookies, looking tender. "He's just a darling, Stella. And very handsome." She patted an almond horn semireverently. "Any boy that knows to bring these . . ."

"And Russian tea cakes and calla lilies," I added.

Mom went a little misty. "I feel like you're growing up in front of my eyes."

"Ew, Mom!" I was afraid she might get like that.

"I can tell he's a serious Catholic."

"Yeah, he is. But not uptight about it."

Mom looked alarmed. "Well, I hope he's a *little* uptight. He hasn't tried to have sex with you, has he?"

"No! Sick! There are some questions you shouldn't ask!"

"Oh no, as your mom, that's a question I *have* to ask."

I jingled the keys. "Much as I was hoping we could talk about how I should stay a virgin forever, I promised I'd go over to Ruby's. She has something important to tell me."

But Mom wasn't finished. "You know, Stella, oral sex counts as sex, too. I heard that a lot of kids don't think so these days, but it does. Don't let anyone try to convince you otherwise."

I mimed puking.

"I'm just trying to watch out for you, honey." Mom waved her hand at me. "Go! Have fun. But remember what I said."

"Mom!"

"I really like him," Mom called as I walked out the door.

I drove fast to Ruby's house, radio at full blast, feeling like I was in a magic bubble. Mike liked Mom; Mom liked Mike.

My life was perfect.

I parked the car and darted up the steps two at a time to knock on Ruby's door.

The door flew open. Ruby was grinning like a maniac. "You took forever!"

I peeled off my jacket and tossed it on the coat tree. "What happened?!"

Ruby let out a repressed squeal. "So I waited at our usual table, right? And he showed up at the same time. The first thing he said was 'You know, you don't have to freeze. I'd give you your hundred dollars just the same if you were sitting inside.' I was, like, 'Good, I'm about to die out here,' so we went inside and sat together in the back. Then he told me his name was Kenneth, and he found out my name, and we just *talked* for, I don't know, an hour. He wanted to know all about me."

"I'll bet he did," I muttered.

Ruby gave me a look. "It turns out he's a graphic designer, and he telecommutes for Microsoft."

"How come he lives in South Bend?"

"It's sad. His mom died, and his dad has Alzheimer's. He's an only child, so he has to stay here and take care of his dad."

"Does he live with him?"

"No, he lives next door. He bought the house just to be near him."

"Wow." I was surprised. Taking care of an elderly parent was not how I imagined this guy. It messed with my one-dimensional notion of pervert. "So he's a graphic designer? For computer programs, or what?"

"He designs the backdrops to video games. How cool is that?"

"Pretty cool," I said, because that's what Ruby wanted to hear.

Privately I was wondering what kind of video games. The ones like Grand Theft Auto, where you get points for having sex with prostitutes and then killing them? The murder spree games where people's heads get blown apart and gray stuff splashes out? I'd seen enough of Marcus's collection to know that few video games were racing simulations anymore.

"He's an *artist*," said Ruby. "He went to Rhode Island School of Design; can you believe that?"

"How did he work that into the conversation?"

"I asked." Ruby narrowed her eyes as if daring me to question him again. Then she went on. "So, he pretty much gets to do what he wants with his time. He works from home and from coffee shops and stuff, and he can take time off whenever. He loves to travel. He's been to every continent."

"He must be pretty loaded."

"He is," Ruby said with relish. "He makes way into the triple digits."

"All this came out in one conversation?"

"We got pretty deep. It was an instant connection, you know? He's basically my dream guy."

"Except he's forty," I said dryly.

"Only thirty-four. Not that I'd have a problem with forty."

"Thirty-four is old, Ruby. It's kind of disgusting."

Ruby raised her eyebrows. "You saw him. Did he look disgusting?"

I had to admit he didn't. He was one of the handsomest men I'd ever seen, but that didn't change the fact that he was practically a senior citizen.

"So then he asked me if I had a job, and I told him no, and—"

"Wait," I interrupted. "Did you tell him you're in high school?"

"No, but he just seemed to know. It was one of the first things he said, actually: 'What are you, about seventeen?' I told him he was the first person to ever get my age right on the first guess."

I started shaking my head. "That's creepy. It's one thing if you lied and he thought you were in your twenties or something. But he *knew* you were seventeen, and he kept talking to you?"

Ruby stared at me. "Are you going to let me finish my story?"

"Yeah, sorry," I said meekly.

"Well, then he asked what kind of grades I got in English, and I told him As; and he asked if I might like a job editing papers for him. He's trying to get some articles published in gaming magazines, and he said he's total crap at punctuation."

"He offered you a job?"

"Yeah, and you're not going to believe how much he's paying me." Ruby grinned smugly. "A hundred dollars an hour."

"One hundred dollars an hour?" It took me a second to process that number. I stared at Ruby, totally weirded out. That was what lawyers made, not what high school kids got paid for random editing jobs.

"It's only on an as-needed basis, but he said I could count on at least a few hours a week."

"Where will you meet? The South Bend Chocolate Company?" My mind was flying ahead: this guy could be dangerous. God forbid he tried to get her to go to his house.

"I don't know; I didn't ask him. But I haven't even told you the best part." Ruby's eyes were dancing. "Close your eyes."

I shut them, baffled.

"Now open them." Ruby was splaying a fan of hundred-dollar bills. "He gave me an advance."

I gasped. "How much is that?"

"A thousand bucks."

"Ruby!" I took one of the bills, checking the texture. It felt and looked real.

"They're real. After he left I stopped at the bank to check."

"That is the most bizarre thing I've ever heard in my life."

Ruby gave an exhilarated sigh. "I know. Now I'm rich, *and* I have a chance to get him to like me. He is seriously my dream guy, Stella. I was setting my standards way too low before."

"Ruby . . ." I didn't know how to put it. Finally I said, "He's so old. This is really weird."

"Oh, you are such a buzz kill." Ruby flicked my arm affectionately. "You know what? Let's go to Trio's for dinner. My treat. You can tell me about Mike meeting your mom."

"Trio's is too expensive; I can't let you pay." But even as I said it, I knew I would. She had just made a thousand dollars. Dinner might cost fifty.

"Shut up, Stel. Let's get decked out and get a fancy bottle of wine and everything."

"I can't drive if I drink."

Ruby rolled her eyes toward heaven. "Stella Chavez! Will you chill? We can get appetizers, dessert, the whole deal. We'll be there at least two hours. A piddly half bottle of wine will wear off in, like, thirty minutes."

"Can I borrow a dress?" I asked, relenting.

"Yeah. I'll do your hair, too. Here, sit. I want to try something new I saw in a magazine. I think it's going to look great on you."

I allowed Ruby to pull me into a chair and run her fingers expertly through my hair, brushing little bits of bangs into my face. "You are so drop-dead gorgeous," she murmured.

"What I would do for this hair."

Well, you couldn't say Ruby wasn't generous with compliments when she was happy. And it was nice to see her excited. But underneath I felt uneasy. This Kenneth thing was insane, clearly a ploy to get into her pants. Talk about Lolita.

I didn't trust him one bit.

Chapter Twelve

After our big dinner at Trio's, which, I had to admit, was super fun, the rest of the weekend melted by quickly. Then it was back to the weekly grind of school and soccer practice and a new, terrifying element: college applications.

They seemed to swoop in out of nowhere, even though I'd been aware of them in the back of my mind. Now it was nearly November, and all of a sudden our teachers, especially our AP teachers, were reminding us that we had just a few months until the admissions deadlines and we should be well on our way to being finished with our essays.

Finished. Ha. I hadn't even started.

I didn't even know where I wanted to apply. I'd been getting glossy college brochures in the mail for months, and they'd been building up in a stack in one of our kitchen drawers. I was feeling massively conflicted about the whole process. To be honest, it had to do with my family. I just couldn't picture them without me. Who would put Marcus to bed when Mom worked late? Who would make sure Jackie got home at a decent hour and didn't wind up in juvie? Who would get the groceries in and the laundry done?

Mom would kill me if she knew I was thinking that way; she'd said a million times that since the only thing our dad left us was a Mexican last name, the least we could do was use it to get a scholarship to a good college. She was under the impression that all Mexicans, black people, and Native Americans could write their ticket to whatever school they wanted and get a full ride.

I tried to tell her it didn't work that way; but she just looked at me hard and said, "Stella, you have great grades, sky-high SAT scores, and you're half Mexican. If you can't make that work for you, you've got issues."

She had a point.

The last thing I wanted was her getting involved in the applications, so I told her not to worry, I had it handled.

But I'd been avoiding thinking about it. The obvious solution was to apply to Notre Dame, St. Mary's, and IUSB so I could live at home while I went to college. But Notre Dame was the only one of those choices that I would be happy with, and it was practically impossible to get in. The school guidance counselor said you had to apply to at least ten schools, anyway, including at least five "safety schools." So far I had three, and two of them I didn't want anything to do with.

Mike jolted me to reality. We were walking around St. Mary's at Notre Dame one afternoon, holding hands and watching the sun sink behind the lake, when he asked, "So where are you applying to college?"

I wasn't expecting it. "Um, University of Phoenix?"

"Seriously."

"I haven't really decided."

Mike was scandalized. "You haven't decided? You have to start early on these things. They're really competitive. You should have started your essays by now."

"I know," I snapped. "That's what everybody keeps telling me."

"Well, do you have a dream school? Like a place you've always wanted to go?"

"Notre Dame?"

Mike beamed and grabbed me in a bear hug. "I was hoping you would say that!" He kissed my neck.

"Mike." I pulled back. "Do you know how hard it is to get into Notre Dame? I probably won't be accepted."

"Yes, you will. You have great grades, you rocked your SATs, and you're local. You'll get in."

"I might not," I said forcefully.

"You *will*. If God wants you to, you will."

Boy, I hated when people said that. Of course it was true, but what if God *didn't* want me to get in? Or what if my college career was too insignificant for God to worry about? That was a distinct possibility, too.

Mike squeezed my hand. "I'll help you with your application. My parents hired a personal admissions counselor for all four years of high school, so I've been through the drill. I know what to do."

I frowned. "A personal admissions counselor? What do they do?"

"Oh, you know: help pick your high school classes, make

sure you do plenty of volunteer work, make sure you're in sports and clubs and stuff. They want you to look well-rounded. They also advise you on where to apply and help you with your essays. They help with SAT prep, too."

I was disgusted. No wonder only rich kids got into the good schools. "How much do they cost?"

"I'm not sure," Mike said thoughtfully. "I never asked."

"Well, I don't belong to any clubs. And I never volunteered anywhere except one week at the nursing home, and then I quit because I couldn't stand the smell of pee."

"You play soccer, don't you?"

"Mike, everybody plays sports."

But he refused to be discouraged. He was so jazzed about the fact that I was applying to Notre Dame that he went off on a tangent about residence halls and the free popcorn and sodas in Coleman-Morse and all the tiny insider details that he could think of to get me excited.

I let him talk while a knot of anxiety formed in my stomach. I hadn't realized some kids had personal admissions counselors. How could I compete with that? And why was I such an idiot that I had never volunteered for anything? Why hadn't I joined student council? Participated in cheesy city cleanups? Rescued abandoned kittens for the SPCA?

"Stella, did you hear what I said?"

"Huh?"

"I said, you're shivering. Do you want to come back to my dorm room and hang out for a while?"

To my surprise, I didn't. Normally I loved curling up on Mike's twin bed, watching TV while he did his homework. His roommate, Kamal, was a quiet Indian boy who spent most of his time studying in the room but left discreetly sometimes so Mike and I could kiss and cuddle.

But tonight I wasn't in the mood. I needed some girl time. Ruby and I hadn't seen each other at all the past week because Ruby had been wrapped up in her "part-time job." I decided to see if she wanted to get coffee, or at least hang out for a while.

Mike was disappointed, but he let me borrow his cell to make plans and then walked me to the visitor parking lot. We kissed good-bye for a while, and finally I had to playfully pry him off and push him away so I could get into my car. He was being extra passionate and intense.

It made me think of Ruby's advice: to say no sometimes, even if you'd had a boyfriend for years, because it keeps them on their toes.

I headed down the familiar winding streets to the Carolines' old Victorian. When Ruby answered the door, she gave me an air kiss on the cheek. That was new: something Kenneth had taught her? "It feels like you haven't been here in forever!"

"I haven't," I agreed. "Well, at least not for the past five days."

"I'm still trying to smoke off the fifty pounds I gained at Trio's." Ruby cinched her hands around her tiny waist.

"I don't think you can smoke off weight. Besides, you're already one pound soaking wet, standing on a scale, holding a wet dog."

"Well, if I smoke I don't eat," Ruby said, looking away to hide how pleased she was at the compliment.

We headed inside the warm house, and I was surprised to see Gina in the kitchen, chopping garlic on a fancy wooden cutting board. "You know how to cook?"

Gina laughed. "Yes, Estelle. You don't have to look so shocked. I'm a rather good cook, actually." She looked like someone out of an urban lifestyle magazine, wearing a black apron, her hair pinned up in a perfect twist, a glass of white wine next to her. An array of colorful produce was lined up on the counter.

"Gina only cooks when she's trying to seduce someone," Ruby explained.

"Ruby!" But Gina didn't look annoyed. In fact, she was glowing.

"Who's the lucky guy?"

"Some suit," Ruby sneered, pulling me by the arm into the hall.

"Is he a jerk or something?" I whispered.

"They're all jerks. Gina loves jerks. The worse they treat her, the more she wants them."

It was the first glimpse Ruby had given me of the internal workings of her home life, and I knew I had to tread carefully. "Why is this one a jerk?"

Ruby shrugged. "I don't know. I haven't met him yet. I'm just going on empirical evidence." She shut the door to her room and turned to face me. Her eyes were dancing with a secret. "Okay, you are not going to believe this. Are you ready?"

"What?"

"Look." She pulled down the top of her green, high-necked sweater and swept aside her hair. A necklace of blackish bruises lined her throat.

I gasped. Ruby smirked, and I caught on. "Hickeys?"

"Kenneth," Ruby mouthed.

"What?! Tell me everything."

Ruby released the neck of her sweater. "He is only the hands-down hottest man I have ever met in my entire life. I'm in love."

I sat on her beanbag. "Start from the beginning."

She perched on the edge of her bed. "Well, so I did a bunch of editing for him last week, right? Then Friday night he wanted to meet so he could look everything over and give me some new stuff to start working on."

"That's a funny time for a meeting."

"Yeah, whatever. I think we both know the editing is a front, right? So I went to his house—"

"His house? He could have raped you!"

"I should be so lucky. Anyway, no woman in the picture. I checked the cabinets and everything. Total bachelor pad."

"Where does he live?"

"You know McAllister? He's a few blocks down from the intersection with Jackson in this cute Victorian. It's kind of like this one, but actually renovated. He has the best taste. So I got there, right? And he answered the door wearing these pants, but no shirt."

"Ruby, it's the dead of winter! What a pervert!"

She shrugged. "Okay, obviously a strategy to show off his pecs, but do I look like I mind? Do you have any idea how good he looked?"

I shook my head wordlessly. Ruby was usually so sharp. I couldn't believe she was taken in by this cheese ball, show-off, dirty old man.

"So he's, like, 'Oh, sorry, I was just changing'; and he pulled on a shirt, and then he took me into the living room and we sat down. He seriously has awesome taste. Like, really exotic, you know? Hangings from South America and masks and stuff. Cool little bongo drums. He has the same incense I do."

I rolled my eyes. "So he shops at Pier One."

"He got me a drink and— "

"Was it alcohol?"

"Yeah, wine. So?"

"Nothing."

"Anyway, he looked over the papers, and he said he couldn't find a single mistake, and he was really impressed with my work, and he wanted to give me another advance. Then he handed me an envelope and told me to count it later."

"How much was in there?"

"Another grand."

"Another grand?" I breathed. "That's disgusting."

"That's not even the good part. He put on this music that was, like, bottled sex or something; and he came over and sat next to me on the couch. There was this really intense moment when he was just looking at me; and he lifted the hair off my neck, and it was so damn sexy I thought I was going to faint. Then he said, 'You're a little tease, you know that?' and he pulled me up and started kissing me *hard*." She touched her neck. "That's when I got these."

"It looks like he tried to strangle you."

"I know, he was biting me and stuff, but it felt amazing."

"Did you have sex with him?"

Ruby looked at me like I was crazy. "Of course not! Don't you know me at all by now?"

I flushed. "Well, yeah, but if he was that hot and everything, I don't know, you might have just done something without thinking about it."

"That would have been stupid. I told you, I'm in *love.* Kenneth could have any girl on the planet. He needs a challenge. No way am I sleeping with him. *Yet.*"

"Ruby . . ." I tried to find a way to say it tactfully. "He might not take you seriously because of the age difference. He obviously thinks you're hot, but it kind of seems like this whole 'job' thing is just a way to get down your pants."

"I know," Ruby said matter-of-factly. "I'm not worried about it. He doesn't take me seriously now, but he will. He's obviously into younger women, right? I just need to get him so out-of-his-brain hot that he can't live without me. I also need to keep him intellectually stimulated. But that shouldn't be a problem."

I gazed at her with a mixture of admiration and worry. She was so confident. But I didn't like those bruises. And something felt very wrong about a thirty-four-year-old man going after a high school girl.

But what if Ruby's right? a voice whispered in my head. *Older men and younger women have been getting together for centuries. Think outside the cultural box.*

There was a soft knock at the door, and Gina stuck her head in the doorway. "Ruby, Brad will be here in half an hour."

Ruby made a face. "It's a school night. Stella has a curfew. Where am I supposed to go?"

"Isn't that coffee place open till late? That's within walking distance."

I tried to hide my shock. Was Gina seriously kicking her out?

"Ruby can spend the night at my house. I'm sure my mom won't mind," I offered quickly.

"Could she? Oh, that would be great. Then I wouldn't have to worry about her getting home safely."

Yeah, you seemed really worried, I thought.

But all I said was "I know it'll be fine. My mom loves Ruby." I'd hoped that last part would give Gina some healthy guilt.

She just looked pleased, though, as she shut the door.

Chapter Thirteen

"My mom and dad want to meet you," Mike told me one evening in his dorm room, his tone carefully casual.

Immediately I was on guard. "What do you mean, they want to meet me?"

"I mean, they want to meet you. They just bought tickets to come visit in March, and they want to take us out to dinner or something. I know it's far in advance, but I thought I'd tell you."

I felt my insides crimp as my head filled with visions of complicated place settings and questions like "What does your father do?" At the same time I was flattered that he was so certain we'd still be together in March. That had to mean something, right?

"Stel? You okay? Don't you want to meet my parents?"

"Yeah." I gave Mike a weak smile. "Of course I do."

"Good."

Was it my imagination, or was the smile he gave me back just as weak? "Have they wanted to meet other girls you dated before?" I asked.

Mike gazed at the ceiling. "Yeah. A few girls in high school, but nobody serious. There was one girl, Elaine, last year; but that didn't last."

This was the first I'd heard of Elaine. "How long were you with her?"

"Um . . . maybe six months."

"That's pretty long. Did your parents like her?"

"Not really. Well, my mom did, but my dad didn't."

"Why?"

"I don't know. My dad has issues." The way Mike said it, I was sure there was something he wasn't telling me.

"Does Elaine go to Notre Dame?" I asked.

"Yeah."

"Is she in any of your classes?"

Mike gave me an irritated look and heaved himself off the bed, where we'd been cuddling. "What is this, the Inquisition?"

My eyes narrowed. "Excuse me?"

"Sorry, I just don't want to talk about her, okay? What's going on with Ruby and the perv, anyway? You haven't given me the 4-1-1 lately."

The expression on his face, and the way he changed the subject, told me all kinds of things I didn't want to know, like maybe he missed this Elaine. And she was definitely in one of his classes.

We didn't talk about it anymore right then, but afterward both Elaine and Mike's parents stuck in my head, nagging at me at random moments. On top of that, school was turning into a total pressure cooker, and I was freaked about starting college applications.

And Ruby was starting to act funny. It wasn't something I could put my finger on; but there was a difference in her, a manic energy and cockiness that went beyond her normal confidence, as if she were riding on top of some big wave, filled with adrenaline. I was worried that at some point she would crash.

We'd gone a few weeks without hanging out after school, both of us wrapped up in our guys, when finally Ruby asked me to spend the night at her house. "I need a girls' night, Stel," she told me one Friday. "You've been ditching me for Mike."

I gaped at her. This was completely untrue. *She* had been ditching *me* for Kenneth.

Ruby saw my look and grinned. "Okay, okay, I've been a little busy with Kenneth, too. You know how it is. The beginning of a relationship, it's kind of intense."

"Yeah," I acknowledged. "Okay, I'm up for a girls' night. Should I bring cute clothes? Are we going out?"

"I don't know. Maybe we should just kick back at home."

I scrutinized her for a moment. There was something odd about the way she said it. "Are you sure?"

"Yeah. We can drink and watch stupid movies. It'll be great. I've been going out too much lately with Kenneth, anyway. I need some downtime."

I shrugged. "Okay."

Later that afternoon we stopped at the grocery store and picked up mixers and a ton of diet foods. Pigging out was inevitable if we were drinking, so Ruby's strategy was to keep all the fattening stuff out of reach. If the only things around were frozen yogurt and baked Lays, we could binge and still stay under a thousand calories.

To my surprise, Gina was home when we got back to Ruby's, lying on the couch with a towel over her eyes and a cigarette in her hand. Her dark hair was pulled into a tight bun, and she wasn't wearing any makeup.

"Is she okay?" I whispered to Ruby as we tiptoed past. The hair and the lack of makeup had me even more worried than the towel and the cigarette.

"The big shot probably dumped her," Ruby whispered back.

"That is *not* what happened," said a hollow voice from the couch.

We both started.

Gina lifted a corner of the towel and narrowed her eyes. "You girls do not understand the complexities of adult relationships."

Ruby snorted. "Oh, right. And you do."

Gina replaced the towel with dignity.

Ruby and I exchanged a glance and headed back to her room. I felt a twinge of delight as I sank into my usual seat: the beanbag chair. It had been weeks since I'd been there, and I hadn't realized how much I'd missed it.

"We have to make a pact to hang out more. We're getting too wrapped up in Mike and Kenneth," I told Ruby, thinking that it was generous of me to say "we."

Ruby nodded as she rummaged through the layer of debris on her floor. "You're right. We can't do that stupid thing girls always do where they let their friendships go because of guys." She produced a crumpled pack of cigarettes triumphantly, shaking one free. "Do you know what Kenneth said the other day?"

"What?"

"He said women are pack animals, and men aren't. He said it's our fundamental difference and the cause of most of the conflict between the sexes."

"That's pretty deep."

Ruby didn't catch my sarcasm. "He's really insightful, you know. I mean, we *are* like pack animals. Except there are only two in my pack." She squeezed my arm, and I couldn't help but grin back.

Then she got up to fight with the sash on the window so she could blow smoke into the yard. I watched her narrow back and the curve of her hips; she was right on that line between too thin and perfect. Did anybody ever look at me objectively and think I was the most beautiful thing they'd ever seen? That's what I saw when I looked at Ruby.

If it were in my nature, I'd be jealous of her, but it wasn't. Mom had taught me that women need to stick together.

Ruby and I lazed away the afternoon like we were twelve, doing manicures and making our way through a series of philosophical questions: What had feminism really done for us? Was perfecting one's weight and appearance a way of taking power or losing it? Was it possible to ever completely trust a man?

The windows eventually darkened, and Ruby poured us drinks. Somewhere she had picked up the idea that as long as you didn't start drinking before sunset, you could give yourself alcohol poisoning and still be socially acceptable.

I sipped my gin and tonic and sank into a comfortable haze. Regardless of Gina, Ruby's house was a place where we could live like adults, doing whatever we wanted. Of course, I knew from Mom that real adulthood was different: it was an endless job of feeding, supporting, and loving kids; wearing shoes till the soles came off; lifting heavy things; and being nice even when you didn't feel like it.

The adulthood that Ruby and I were playing at was more of a glamorous interlude between adolescence and the real thing. This made it even more precious: a witching hour of our lives when anything was possible.

Ruby clicked an ice cube against her teeth and asked, "How are things with you and Mike?"

"I'm meeting his parents when they come up in March."

"Oooh-la-la. Meeting the parents."

"Yeah, except they're these loaded bigwigs. They'll probably think I'm trying to trap Mike in an unequal marriage or something."

"Isn't it a little early to be talking about marriage?"

I was embarrassed; she caught me.

Ruby looked at me closely. "Are *you* thinking about marriage?"

"No! It was just a figure of speech."

"Uh-huh. Well, I wouldn't worry about them. I'll help you with your outfit, and you can read some nineteenth-century book on manners, and you'll be fine."

I perked up. "Do you really think there's a book on manners for these situations?"

"There's a book on everything." Ruby raked through the clothing pile next to her and picked up a black sheath dress. "Add pearls, and voilà: instant class."

There was a knock at the door, and Gina peered in. I froze from reflex, horribly conscious of the bottle of gin on the floor; but she didn't seem to notice. She was fully made up now, her hair in an elegant upsweep, and wearing a daring red dress. "I'm going out," she said.

"Have fun," said Ruby.

Gina closed the door, and a few minutes later we heard the front door bang and the car purr to life.

"She'll go to LaSalle and wait for the next lawyer or doctor or exec to hit on her," said Ruby. "It's her way of recovering."

"From getting dumped?"

"Yes."

"But how do you know for sure she got dumped?"

"Because it happens *every single time*." Ruby got to her feet. "We've been sitting too long. You want to have some fun?"

"Sure. What are we doing?"

"You'll see." She pulled a few jackets from the mess, tossing one in my direction. Then she rummaged in the makeup bag on her dresser.

"What do you have in there? Are we going out somewhere?"

"I said, you'll see." Ruby opened the door and led the way down the hall to Gina's room. It was the only room in the house I'd never seen, and I was more than a little curious as we stepped inside. The bed had a big, dark-wood headboard and a maroon comforter. Silky gray throw pillows, detailed with flame-colored beads, were arranged on the covers just so. The bedside tables held glass lamps with pale gray shades. A huge mirror leaned against one wall, trimmed in black and gray with white glass squares. Everything was sexy and striking without being overdone.

"Wow," I breathed, taking it in.

Ruby was busy in the corner, fiddling with something on the wall.

"What's that?" I asked.

"Stairs to the roof. You just have to get them out." Ruby gave a sharp jerk, and a panel slid open to reveal a narrow set of stairs leading into the ceiling. She started to climb. "All these old houses have them. Come on."

I followed her, gazing up in wonder as she unlatched a rectangular door in the ceiling and pushed. A draft of cold air swept my face. Ruby climbed through and hoisted herself out. I followed, giddy, laughing as my head emerged into the night air and the whole sky full of stars opened up around me. Ruby helped me climb out; and we stood on the roof, heads tipped back, drinking in the sky.

"Isn't it amazing up here?" Ruby's breath fogged the air.

I nodded. The stars were brilliant. Names I'd learned in elementary school jumped into my head: Betelgeuse, Orion, the Milky Way.

Ruby started across the roof. "You get the best view over here."

I followed her but lingered a few feet back while she made her way to the very edge.

"Come on, Stel, you chicken?"

"No, you're crazy." I had never been big on heights; and being tipsy, I wasn't about to start now. It made me nervous that Ruby's toes were nearly touching the line where the roof dropped into the gutter.

She tossed back her head and lifted her arms up to the sky, and for one awful moment I thought she was going to jump.

"Ruby!" My voice came out in a hoarse croak, and she turned to laugh at me.

"Did you think I was going to jump?"

"No."

"Don't be crazy. I would never jump." She came back to join me and sank to her knees, emptying her pockets onto the dark shingles. A compact, a little bag, a razor blade. She opened the bag and carefully tapped some white powder onto the open compact.

I finally caught on. Tension coiled in the pit of my stomach. Coke was too much. Coke was trashy Tiffany Zimmerman who went to rehab. Coke was your septum rotting.

Coke was why I lost my dad.

I watched silently as Ruby sliced the powder into lines and fished a dollar bill from her pocket. I felt a pang of gray humor, remembering her joke when I'd asked her, months ago, what we would do in Chicago: "Snort coke through dollar bills and dance in G-strings for hot stockbrokers."

Ruby offered me the little mirror, and I shook my head.

"Your loss." She ducked her head and snorted two of the lines. Then she set the compact on the roof and leaned back on her arms, breathing deeply and staring into the net of lights over downtown.

I had to ask. "When did you start doing coke?"

Ruby gave me an irritated glance. "Don't get preachy on me. It's really not that big of a deal."

"Kenneth?"

"I'm not going to answer that." She stared out at the city, brooding; but her mood changed like quicksilver, and she reached over to touch my arm, her eyes glittering like a cat's. "I think I'm in love. Like the real thing."

"You do?"

She nodded. "He makes me feel powerful and weak at the same time, and it's so sexy. He's like a dark angel. Like Lucifer in that one book . . . oh, I forget the name. *Paradise* whatever. He always gets what he wants, you know that? He says if he envisions it the right way, it just happens. He says we create our own reality. Do you believe that?"

I shivered at the comparison to Lucifer. "No."

"Why not? He says if you focus your energy, anything can happen. That's how he met me."

"He focused his energy on you?"

Ruby shrugged. "He focused his energy on finding a woman who fit my description."

"Seventeen and hot? That's real original."

Ruby shoved me, but without malice. "I'll tell you another one. He envisioned getting this great job that pays in the triple digits, and it happened."

"What do you think he'll 'focus his energy on' next?"

"I don't know; but whatever it is, he'll get it."

"Ruby, that's creepy."

Ruby laughed, and I could see the coke like a veil over her face, artificial and arrogant and cold. She lit a cigarette and took a long, hungry drag. Her teeth were chattering. "Why not? If you could have whatever you wanted, wouldn't you take it?"

I thought about it for a minute. "No."

Ruby snorted. "Tell me one thing you want but you wouldn't take."

"Sometimes we want things that aren't good for us," I

retorted. "Only God knows what we really need."

"God, huh? Well, you certainly know how to dump a bucket of ice water on a conversation." Ruby got to her feet and stood, staring into the sky and chain-smoking. When she finally spoke again, her comment was the last thing in the world I expected. "Do you think Gina's prettier than me?"

I stared at her. "You're . . . you're not even in the same ballpark! Gina's like in her forties! Yeah, she's beautiful, but she's old."

"So you think I'm prettier?"

"It's like comparing apples and oranges!" I saw the look on her face and added, "But yeah, of course you're prettier. Why?"

Ruby gestured fiercely with her cigarette. "Because she always gets dumped. If she's so beautiful, how come she always gets dumped?"

"Oh, Ruby." I stood up and put my arm around her shoulders; but she stiffened, and I quickly pulled back. She tossed a smoldering butt onto the roof, and I stamped it out. "Come on. Let's go inside," I said.

"Hold on. Let me finish this."

I watched as Ruby snorted the last line, wiping up the traces of powder and rubbing them into her gums.

This Kenneth. I wanted to kill him.

I made sure Ruby went down the ladder first and then followed her, pulling the trapdoor shut behind me. We headed to her room and I sat down, feeling kind of sad and tired.

Ruby started sorting through her clothes, tossing dresses onto the bed and fishing jewelry from the heap that she kept on top of her nightstand. "This one is so pretty, but it always rides up on the legs. . . . I wish I didn't have so many black dresses. . . . What do you think about this one; no, this one?" Ruby chattered in a hyped-up stream of consciousness, holding various dresses against her body. "I think we should go out. Let's go out, Stella. To hell with Kenneth."

I glanced at her. "What do you mean, 'to hell with Kenneth'? I thought you were in love with him."

She draped a rope of green glass beads around her neck and held up matching earrings. "Are these tacky? Or cool?"

"They're pretty. What did you mean about Kenneth?"

She sighed. "He's protective. Can't handle it when I'm all dressed up without him. He gets jealous."

"Has he asked you not to go out?"

"Nooo . . . well, kind of. He didn't say it, but he made it pretty obvious. I like these better. They're classier." Ruby held out some amber beads. "Yeah?"

"Yeah. How did he make it obvious?"

"Okay, Detective Chavez."

I flinched. Twice now this week I'd been accused of being nosy.

"He is *not* controlling me, if that's what you're wondering. I like it that he's protective. It's a sign he really cares."

"Or that he's psycho," I pointed out.

But Ruby wasn't offended. "I like 'em a little psycho," she said with a wicked grin. "Anyway, we have to go out. I'm too high to stay inside right now. I need a dance floor." She spread her arms and shimmied, giggling.

I didn't feel like laughing. "I'm tired."

"Stel, come on! *Please.*"

But I didn't like the cute sound in her voice or her pleading, persuasive look. Everything was fake right now; everything was coke.

"I'm really tired. Let's go out a different night."

"You are so boring!" Ruby pouted. But she tossed the beads back onto the table.

"Let's watch one of the movies we got," I suggested.

"But I need to *move*."

"So tap your feet." I stood up. "I'm going to watch a movie. You don't have to if you don't want to."

"You're annoyed that I'm high," Ruby said knowingly as she followed me down the hall. "That's okay. Coke wears off fast."

"Good." I grabbed the remote and the stack of DVDs. I wasn't in the mood to talk.

Chapter Fourteen

Ironically, it was Ruby who made me start my college applications.

After the whole lines-on-the-roof incident, things were a
little cool between us. It made me feel sick inside—furious and
disgusted—and I knew a lot of that was because of my dad.
I didn't care that she smoked and drank a lot, but coke was
crossing the line.

Predictably, Ruby picked up on my distance and turned on
the charm. "Let's go to South Bend Chocolate Company. No
Mike, no Kenneth, just us," she suggested Thursday afternoon.

"I have soccer," I started.

"You can't miss one practice? Come on. I won't even
smoke." She said it like such a martyr that I couldn't help
smiling. "Besides, I have something for you."

"What, heroin?"

Ruby looked startled, then laughed. "Nice, Stella. You're

getting an edge. No, something much more wholesome."

Cutting soccer didn't sound half bad. Ever since the big confrontation, Christine and Brianna treated me like I didn't exist during practice. It was horrible to have them—especially Christine—pass me the ball but refuse to meet my eyes. As if our ten years of friendship had never happened. Brianna I could ignore, but Christine I wanted to shake and say, "Are you serious? Can we forget this and move on?"

But I was paralyzed; and the longer it went on, the more permanent it seemed.

So I said to Ruby that the Chocolate Company sounded good, and we headed off when the bell rang. The coke thing kept nagging at the back of my mind, but I told myself that I should have expected it. This was Ruby. What on earth made me think she *wouldn't* do coke? Or anything else on God's green earth, for that matter? Wasn't her sense of adventure one of the things I loved most about her?

When we got to the café, we ordered our usual and sat in a comfy corner indoors. Ruby was pointedly not smoking for me. As soon as we got settled, she rummaged through her purse and pulled out a sheaf of papers, setting them on the table with a flourish.

"What are those?" I asked.

"Look and see." She leaned back and watched as I pulled the pile toward me. The top paper had a gold header with the Notre Dame insignia. It was covered with small print and empty lines.

"You got me a college application?" I asked incredulously.

"Yeah. I would have gotten more, but I don't know where else you want to apply. We can download them; you just have to tell me where you want to go."

"Ruby . . ." I gestured helplessly at the pile, touched that she had gone to all that trouble. "Are you my mom now or something?"

She fixed me with a hard stare. "No, but your mom would freak out if she knew you hadn't even started a single application. Do you want to be one of those stupid people who doesn't even have it together enough to get into college?"

As always, Ruby's double standard left me stunned. "What about you?"

"I'll be fine."

"Oh, yeah, right! Tell me one application you've finished!"

"I'm not going to college next year."

"What?"

"I said, I'm not going to college next year. But with me it's a decision. With you it would be an accident that you let happen."

"What do you mean you're not going to college next year? Why?"

"Kenneth and I are going to Asia in September and October. I can't miss the first two months of school, so I'll just start the year after that." She grinned. "My admissions essays will probably be a lot more interesting that way, anyhow."

"You . . ." I petered out. "He's taking you to *Asia*?"

"Yeah. We're going to climb the old temples, and hike the mountains, and eat crazy sushi, and stay in five-star hotels, and ride that famous train—you know, the Orient Express? I can't wait. He showed me all the brochures. They're not weird about age over there the way they are in this country."

"How come you didn't tell me?"

"Because you don't like Kenneth. I figured you'd be all negative and try to talk me out of it."

We stared at each other. I knew she was right, but I still felt betrayed.

Ruby looked defiant. "Do you know how bad it feels that my best friend hates the guy I'm in love with? Every time I talk about him you say something snotty or get all quiet."

I cut hard into my dessert and stared at my plate. I had never considered this thing from Ruby's angle. She was right, of course. I mean, I still thought Kenneth was a pervy lecher, but it wasn't her fault she'd fallen for him. She was practically programmed that way, from what I could tell. And here I was, her best friend—her only friend, really—not even letting her be all giddy.

"You're right," I muttered. "Sorry."

Ruby's tone softened. "You guys should get to know each other. Maybe we could all go out to dinner or something."

That sounded almost as fun as meeting Mike's parents, but I smiled tightly. "Okay. Let's do it."

"But you'll have to dress kind of boring," Ruby added. "Nothing low cut. I don't want him checking you out."

"Ruby, he's met me twice, and he has no idea I exist. Both times I saw him, he couldn't take his eyes off you. I don't think you have anything to worry about."

"Really? He couldn't take his eyes off me?"

I rolled my eyes. "Come on. Don't act like you don't know it."

"Well, it's still nice to hear." Ruby reached across the table and shoved the application an inch closer. "You better actually do these or I swear I'll tell your mom."

"You wouldn't."

"I would."

I half believed her.

I evened out the stack of pages and tucked it in my bag. Part of me was relieved that she was kicking me into gear. I had been feeling weighed down and helpless about the whole thing, and it was getting worse every day. Now I would actually have to do something about it.

Chapter Fifteen

It's a good thing Ruby forced the application on me, because it was harder than I thought. There were all kinds of random things to fill out, including a lot of information about my dad that I had to leave blank. You'd think there were enough single-parent families out there that there'd be a No Dad box to check, but there wasn't.

That part was a picnic, though, compared to the essay questions. Notre Dame had six, and I was allowed two hundred and fifty words for each. They included awful, probing ones like "How would you describe yourself as a human being?" and "Write about a difficulty in your past that has helped form who you are today."

I got into a daily grind of staring at my computer screen with a giant mug of coffee in hand and Pi curled up on my lap, trying to figure out how to answer the unanswerable.

The whole process gave me the munchies, sweats, and

insomnia, and also used up most of my Christmas vacation. Mom was working all the time anyway, so it wasn't like I missed out on family time, but it would have been nice to relax a little.

Christmas itself *was* nice, though: Mom had both Christmas Eve and Christmas Day off for the first time in years; and we went to Midnight Mass, opened presents the next morning, and had a "pass-the-pass-the." That's what we call meals where we actually sit down and pass dishes along the table. It was cool to have a full forty-eight hours together. Most people hate being around their parents, but in our family it was the opposite: it felt like a special treat, a magic ingredient that made me, Jackie, and Marcus belong in the same recipe.

Of course, it wouldn't be a holiday without some family drama. It happened after dinner when we were all vegging out in the living room, watching a movie. Mom had cranked up the heater past our usual money-saving sixty-five, and it was getting warm. Jackie took off her sweater. Her hair was pulled back in a ponytail, and my eyes were drawn instantly to a black scrawl on the back of her neck.

"Did you get a *tattoo*?" I asked.

"No!" Jackie tore the elastic band out of her ponytail, and her hair cascaded down her back. But it was too late.

"I cannot *believe* you got a tattoo." I looked at Mom for support.

"Jackie, is that a tattoo?" Mom's mild tone didn't fool anyone. She was not a fan of tattoos, and we all knew there would be a major freak-out if one of us got one.

"It's just a drawing." Jackie pulled her hair aside to prove it, and Mom and I both leaned in for a look.

It was weird—an *A* in a circle. I felt like I'd seen it someplace before. Maybe on the walls of our school.

"Is that a *gang* sign?" I asked, slightly hysterical.

"No!" Jackie snapped. "You're so *paranoid!*"

"Jackie, your sister cares about you. Why don't you just tell us what it is, and nobody will bother you about it anymore."

I could practically see the cogs spinning in Jackie's head. "It's an initial," she said after a pause. "Of a guy I like."

Mom smiled. "Oh, honey. Do you want to tell us about him?"

"No," said Jackie.

"Mom, are you seriously going to fall for that?" I demanded.

Jackie glared at me, and Mom said with dignity, "I'm going to accept your sister's word for it, Stella. And I think you should, too."

That burned me. But Mom had closed the case, and there wasn't a thing I could do about it.

Jackie shot me a triumphant look as she turned back to the TV.

I didn't say anything about it after that. But I decided to keep an extraclose eye on DaShawn and his crew.

By December 26 I was back at writing. When I finally finished a stack of drafts, I was in bad shape: exhausted and uptight, with about five pounds of Christmas cookies pasted to my thighs. I no longer had any perspective on anything I'd written.

I decided to show the essays to Mike since he'd gone through the process himself and had been accepted. Friday night I took them to his dorm.

Mike was watching TV and lounging on his bed in a fitted long-sleeved T-shirt and distressed jeans. We hadn't seen each other all week since he'd been gone for Christmas.

"Hey, Abercrombie & Fitch," I said from the doorway.

"Stella!" He jumped up and gathered me in a big hug, kissing the top of my head. "Hand them over!"

I handed him the sheaf of papers, feeling awkward, and curled up on his bed. He tried to flop down next to me, but I held out a hand to block him. "I can't watch you read them. It'll drive me crazy."

"Whatever." He stole a quick kiss and went to his desk to look them over.

I tried to watch TV; but it was ESPN, and I could barely process what was happening on the screen. I kept sneaking glances at Mike, hoping to catch some kind of positive expression on his face. Impressed? Touched? Interested?

Instead, he looked . . . skeptical. "Well, you're a good writer," he finally said, setting down the stack. He didn't sound convinced.

"You're lying."

"No, you are a pretty good writer. But I think you're taking the wrong angle on a couple of these."

"Like which ones?"

"Well, mostly the difficulty one. It sounds like a sob story."

I was shocked. It was one of those moments when the wrongness just swells and fills the room. "What do you mean?"

"I mean, I don't know; I'm not sure they'll even believe it.

It's kind of soap opera-ish, you know?"

"It's my life."

"Well, yeah, I know. But the most important thing is how Admissions will perceive it, right?"

I stared at two football players crashing into each other on the screen as a red wave of resentment grew inside me. I had written about how my dad emptied our bank account to go on a drug binge with a couple of his buddies, maxed out all our credit cards, and then disappeared. I described how Mom went to look for a second job the week after he left even though she could barely hold herself together. I wrote how I knew, at age ten, that I was going to have to take Dad's place. And that I did. I helped raise Jackie, who was seven, and Marcus, who was three, all the way until now.

"Fuck you," I whispered under my breath.

"What?"

"Nothing," I muttered. He wouldn't understand.

Mike looked concerned. "Look, babe, I know this stuff happened. I'm not saying it was easy. Don't be mad at me. I'm just trying to help you get in."

"I know," I snapped. Mike's mom's "job" was to buy home decor and throw parties. Their family had more cars than people. They had pet charities, went to Paris as if it were the next town over. These were details that had come out over the course of many conversations, and I was remembering them now. Thinking about what they meant for the two of us.

"Stel?" Mike sat down next to me.

I imagined a thin metal barrier between us, cold and impermeable.

"I thought you wanted me to critique them."

"I did." Too bad I was totally regretting it.

"Well, I think the others are awesome. I wouldn't change a thing. Seriously." His voice sounded fake. Of course, now he was probably scared to tell me anything; I bet he thought I was one of those idiots who couldn't handle criticism.

I wanted to tell him that wasn't it at all—it was much bigger than that—but the words wouldn't come out.

"Are you mad?"

"No, not really." I forced a smile, and he looked relieved.

"Listen, with those SAT scores, you're getting in. No question."

"Yeah, well."

He set my papers on his desk and squeezed onto the twin bed, which was really too small to hold both of us. I let him take my hand and cuddle close, but the barrier was still there.

"You know, my parents are really excited to meet you."

It was obviously a peace offering, but I couldn't think of anything I wanted to hear less at the moment. "That's nice."

"They want to take us to Tippecanoe. It's South Bend's version of fancy."

South Bend's version of fancy? Did he realize how stuck-up he sounded?

I climbed over him and stood up. I was full of poison at the moment, and I realized dimly that I wasn't being fair. "I should go. I want to make sure I'm home when Marcus and Jackie get there. They've been on their own a lot lately."

Mike looked startled. "You've only been here, like, half an hour. I haven't seen you in a week!"

"I'm sorry. I should have planned better."

"You're still mad, aren't you?" He stared me down.

"No," I lied.

"Will I see you tomorrow?"

"Okay."

"Come over after soccer practice?"

I nodded.

"Don't forget your essays."

I turned to pick them up from his desk. I should have known better than to write about something that actually mattered. I should have made up something, like so many other kids I knew. Something about Mexican identity and immigration. My youth in the orange groves.

"Stel, are you sure you're okay?" Mike's face was worried.

"Yeah, I'm fine." I gave him a bright smile. "See you tomorrow."

I left without kissing him good-bye.

Chapter Sixteen

A few days later I turned in my Notre Dame application directly to the Office of Admissions. On the way to drop it off, I veered into the women's bathroom and took the application out to check for the millionth time that all the papers were in order. Then I said a prayer and made the sign of the cross over the packet.

It hit me suddenly how stupid it was to apply to just one school.

But it was too late to apply to any more, at least not to top-tier colleges; and those were the only ones I was interested in. I was doing this for Mom and Jackie and Marcus, I told myself, trying to push down my anxiety. They needed me around.

I wasn't sure where to drop the envelope, so I had to wait in line at Admissions, which gave me more time to obsess.

I had rewritten my "difficulty" essay question like Mike had suggested, and I was starting to wonder if that was a mistake.

My new version was safe: a story about how going on wilderness camp sophomore year had helped me overcome shyness. It was the kind of thing I thought a well-rounded, upper-middle-class white girl might consider a "difficulty." And that was what they were looking for, right? A white girl in Latina skin, a nice fit with campus culture *and* good for their demographics?

It definitely wasn't "soap-operaish," anyway.

When I handed the packet to the receptionist, I should have felt relief. But instead my stress ratcheted up. There were no more chances to revise. No safety schools waiting in the wings to accept me if I completely messed this up.

I headed out of the building and walked a quick lap around St. Joseph's Lake to decompress. The air was biting, frost sparkled on the branches, and the lake was dotted with dark patches of ice. It would probably be frozen through in a few weeks.

After walking around the lake I made my way back through the quad, hands plugged into my pockets to keep warm. Students were hurrying on the diagonal walkways, clutching paper coffee cups, cheeks and noses red from cold. Could this be me next year, carrying a bag full of textbooks, going home to one of those beautiful old dorms?

Probably not. The thought was like a tumor gnawing at my brain.

I glanced at Mike's dorm as I passed. I just couldn't handle seeing him at the moment. He had apologized again about the essay comment, and I had forgiven him—I knew he was only trying to help—but I couldn't shake the feeling that we were more different than I'd realized.

Ruby was who I needed to see, I decided. She always put things into perspective. Feeling guilty about avoiding Mike, I got into my car and headed for Juniper Street.

Ruby was out front, smoking. She grinned and waved as I got out of the car.

A moment later I sat down next to her and helped myself to a cigarette. Her eyebrows shot up, but she didn't say anything, which I appreciated. I lit the cigarette, took a drag, and winced. "These things are disgusting. How do you smoke them?"

"Acquired taste. Don't start. They'll give you cancer."

"What about you?"

Ruby shrugged. "You only live once." As usual, her hypocrisy amazed and sort of inspired me.

"Maybe I need a drink in order to make it taste okay."

"You badass! Hold on and I'll get you something. Then you're telling me what's going on." Ruby disappeared into the house. I stared at the Golden Dome of Notre Dame peeking above the trees and took another puff. Smoking really was disgusting. I stabbed the cigarette out.

The porch creaked behind me. "Here." Ruby thrust a glass clinking with ice cubes into my hand. "Take it slow. It's mostly whiskey."

I took a sip. "This doesn't even taste like something you should drink. It's more like cleaning fluid or something."

"Well, whole countries beg to differ. Now tell me what's going on."

"Nothing you don't already know. It's just kicking in that I probably won't go to college next year."

"Because you only applied to Notre Dame?" Ruby guessed.

I nodded grimly. She was the only one I could admit it to. "I could have applied to St. Mary's and IUSB or even Valparaiso, but I was being a snob."

"Or Harvard or Columbia or wherever you wanted," Ruby added.

I shot her a resentful look. "No, I couldn't. And you know why, so don't even go there."

"Actually, I think you *should* go there. I mean, when is it going to be okay to leave South Bend? When Jackie and Marcus are in their thirties?"

Ruby's question hit me. I started to babble. "Look, I know you think I'm being a martyr, but DaShawn Green is hanging around Jackie, and he's supposed to be a Blood or something, and you know he smokes blunts like they're freaking beadies, and she drew this weird thing on her neck that could have been a gang sign for all I know. How can I trust her to take care of herself, let alone make sure Marcus does his homework and eats something besides Lucky Charms and—"

"Like you and I haven't had our share of adventures," Ruby cut me off gently. "And isn't Jackie wicked smart? Weren't you bragging about her PSATs a few months ago?"

"Smart doesn't stop you from doing stupid stuff. I already lost one person in my family. I don't want to lose someone else," I blurted.

And in that instant I realized something: Jackie reminded me of my dad. Dad before he got sick, when he was fiery and fun and could make cashiers laugh over nothing, then five minutes later throw a look that made people step out of our way on the sidewalk.

"That's fair. I get it," Ruby said. We were quiet for a few minutes. Then, with a true friend's instinct for when to change the subject, she asked, "So what's up with Mike?"

That was easier. I took another drink. The whiskey was starting to smooth me out. "I don't know. I'm not sure I'm in love with him."

"If you're not sure, that means you're not. If you're in love, you know it."

I glanced at Ruby enviously. Why hadn't I ever felt as crazy passionate about someone as she did for Kenneth?

"Love is intense," she said as if she'd caught Kenneth vibes in the air. "It's this red-hot spark that makes you out of your mind for the other person, like you're not living unless you're with them. It's all encompassing. It erases you."

"I don't know if I'd like that."

"In a good way, silly. It erases you and melts you with the person so you're part of the same entity."

"Sounds pretty metaphysical."

Ruby elbowed me in the side. "Quit it. I'm serious."

I knew she was, but she'd lost me on that last part. I wanted to stay me, no matter what. Maybe that's why I never liked getting drunk.

"I don't know. The couples I know that have pretty good marriages don't seem red-hot. They seem more like best friends." I thought of Christine's parents and some of my mom's friends from church. "I mean, you don't get a sense they have a sizzling sex life. But maybe they do. I don't know."

"Maybe they keep it behind closed doors," Ruby said. "Or maybe they're not really in love, and they don't know what they're missing."

"I think you're getting love mixed up with passion."

Ruby looked annoyed. "Well, then I'd rather have passion any day."

For some reason, that made me sad.

I thought of beautiful Gina with her brave red dress. Then I thought of Christine's mom, dumpy Mrs. Blair in her sweat suits, and how Mr. Blair always looked at her as if she were some kind of queen. "I think I'd rather have love," I said.

Ruby stood abruptly. "It's getting cold. You want to go in?"

I stood, feeling dizzy. "Sorry."

"For what?"

"I didn't mean to be obnoxious. I think it's great you and Kenneth have both."

Ruby softened immediately. "Thanks. He's amazing."

"What's so amazing about him?" I really wanted to know.

"Well, besides the sexiness and all, he's such a good person. I mean, he's living in this backwater place just to take care of his dad, even though he could be telecommuting from anywhere he wants."

"His dad has Alzheimer's, right?"

"Yeah. Sometimes he doesn't even know who Kenneth is."

"Has he introduced you?"

Ruby shook her head. "Kenneth said it would confuse him." As we walked into the house, she added, "Remember I said we should all go out for dinner or something? Well, I'm meeting Kenneth at LaSalle for drinks tonight. You want to come?"

"Do you think he'll care if I'm there?"

"Why would he? He should want to meet my friends."

But Ruby sounded uncertain.

"Maybe he won't want a third wheel."

"We get plenty of alone time, believe me. I think it's time he got to know you. And maybe Gina, too, but not tonight. One at a time is enough."

"Gina?" I echoed.

"Yeah." Ruby looked worried. "You don't think he'll be attracted to her or anything, do you?"

"No! Are you crazy? But don't you think Gina will be upset that you're dating a full-grown man? I mean, I know she's pretty chill, but come on."

"We have to come out of the closet at some point. I'm almost eighteen. What's she going to do?"

"Call the cops?"

Ruby snorted. "You don't know Gina. She would never call the cops. She might lecture me, but probably not even that. She really won't care that much, Stella."

Again I got a sad feeling. Because I was pretty sure Ruby was right.

Ruby pulled a bag of sugar-free Godiva squares from the cupboard and rustled them at me. "Fifteen calories each and no gross aftertaste. We can eat these while we're getting ready."

I grinned at her. This was one of the things I loved about Ruby: her ability to inject fun into everything. She was my antidote.

I followed her to the bedroom to get ready, leaving my drink in the kitchen. I needed to be sharp if I was going to hang out with Kenneth properly for the first time.

Chapter Seventeen

I felt like a total impostor at Club LaSalle.

For one thing, we had to be the youngest there by at least fifteen years. Most of the people were dressed like they were going to work. The women had careful highlights, low heels. The men were stocky and balding. Everyone looked alarmingly parentlike. The only exception was a group of hippie-ish older women, who were clearly on their third or fourth round of drinks, talking at the top of their lungs about somebody named Foo-koe.

The lounge was formal, done in brown leather and heavy carpeting. The faint, spicy odor of cigars clung to the air. The bar was a horseshoe in the center of the room; and a small, round man who looked like an owl was standing in the center, polishing a wineglass with a cloth. His head swiveled the moment we walked in, and his eyebrows rose. It was a clear message: don't even try.

"Ruby, we have to go," I whispered.

"Huh?"

"That guy isn't going to let us stay."

"Who? Gregory? I'll handle it." Ruby breezed right up to the bar. I followed, but stayed back a few feet. Though Ruby was leaning against the bar, obviously waiting for him, Gregory took his time finishing the glass and placing it on a shelf. He snapped the towel onto a hook and went to collect several empties from a group of men. Finally, after putting them in a dishwasher, he walked over to Ruby.

"Hi, Gregory. Has Kenneth come in yet?"

"No."

"Two gin and tonics, please. You can start a tab for Kenneth."

For a moment Ruby and Gregory stared at each other over the bar. Then, with what sounded like a snort, Gregory grabbed two glasses and violently dunked them in ice, poured about half a shot of gin in each, and filled the rest with tonic. He shoved them toward Ruby and whirled around, busying himself at the cash register.

Ruby took a sip of her drink and sighed. "Gregory?"

He didn't turn around.

I clutched her arm and hissed, "What are you doing? He's going to kick us out."

"He won't kick us out." Then, louder, "Gregory? These are a little weak. Could you please add some more gin?"

I stifled a groan.

With a frozen expression, Gregory poured the tiniest drop of extra gin in Ruby's glass and pushed it toward her.

To my huge relief, she didn't complain. She just collected

our drinks and nodded toward one of the free couches. "You want to sit over there? I think Gregory would feel better if we got out of his face."

"How did you get away with that?" I asked as we walked away.

"Kenneth is practically best friends with Phil, the owner. When Gregory said he wasn't sure if my ID was legit, Phil gave him a warning."

"Yeah, but if Gregory gets busted then he's in trouble, not Phil."

"No, Phil has to pay a fine, too. But come on. Gregory knows I'm not a sting; he's just being uptight." Ruby took a sip of her drink and wrinkled her nose. "Still weak. I'll have to get Kenneth to fix it when he gets here."

I sighed and leaned back into the cool leather. I was wearing one of Ruby's dresses: a plum-colored, V-necked thing that made me feel like a society wife. Ruby seemed right at home in her brown dress with pearls. She was like a chameleon.

"There he is." She tucked a strand of hair behind her ear and straightened. From my vantage point I could see Kenneth as he approached—and the look of surprise that flitted across his face when he saw me at the table.

"Hi." He folded his jacket neatly over the edge of the couch and sat next to Ruby, smoothing his pant legs. He was wearing chinos and a white button-down shirt, obviously expensive material. From head to toe he was perfectly groomed: silver hair carefully tousled, leather shoes gleaming, nails trimmed and shiny. Was it possible he got manicures?

His eyes played over me, and I was surprised at how little I could read of his expression. It gave me a weird feeling.

"You met Stella before at the Chocolate Company, remember? I thought it would be fun if she had a drink with us." Ruby sounded nervous.

"Well, nice to see you again, Stella. I'm glad you can join us." Kenneth showed his perfect teeth.

"Nice to see you again, too." There was a pause, the beginning of an awkward silence, and Ruby pushed her glass toward Kenneth.

"Gregory's being stingy with the gin again. Will you make him fix it?"

"You're going to send the man to an early grave." Kenneth grinned, but he took the glass and stood, then scooped up mine, too. "I take it yours probably has the same issue?"

"No, mine's okay. I don't like it too strong."

"Hmm. Knowing Gregory, it isn't even middling." Kenneth kept both glasses and walked toward the bar. I was annoyed. I hadn't wanted a stiff drink; I'd had plenty earlier.

Ruby shredded a strip off her cocktail napkin.

"You okay?" I asked.

She nodded. "I just want you guys to like each other."

"I'm sure we'll get along fine." It was the best I could do without flat-out lying. How did she not see this guy was oozing slime from every pore?

Kenneth was back quickly, our drinks in one hand and a glass of something amber-colored in the other. He set them on the table in front of us. "These should be better."

Ruby took a sip. "I think he got revenge by putting in too much this time."

"Well, call it a martini, then." Kenneth leaned back next to her, cradling his drink between both hands. He tilted his head against the seat. "Long day. How about you girls?" It was a relaxed pose and a relaxed comment, but there was something tense about him. His eyes were so sharp, you could tell he didn't miss a thing.

"Pretty good. I put the ACE bandage on like you said, and I didn't even feel my knee when I went jogging this morning," Ruby said.

I looked at her in surprise. "I didn't know you jogged."

"I encouraged her to start," said Kenneth. "Helps her stay slim."

"I actually really like it," said Ruby. "But I have these bad joints, so Kenneth got me some supplements and the bandage, and I don't even feel them anymore."

"Glucosamine and chondroitin. They work wonders," said Kenneth.

"Are you a runner, too?" I asked.

"Three miles every morning. I lift weights a couple times a week, too." He flexed jokingly, but enough to show the bulge of muscle through his shirt. "How about you, Stella? You look like you work out." His eyes skimmed my figure as if he was examining a piece of merchandise. "Soccer or ballet?"

"Yeah, soccer," I said grudgingly.

Kenneth nodded. "You can always tell by the legs." A funny look crossed Ruby's face, and Kenneth caught it. He squeezed her thigh. "Honey, just so you know; there's only one pair of legs that I'm interested in at the moment. I used to be a personal trainer; I can't help but notice people's physiques."

"I didn't know you used to be a personal trainer, too," Ruby said admiringly.

"Oh yeah, back in college. Pocket money." For some reason

Kenneth looked uncomfortable. "Well, and what else were you two up to today?"

"Just high school as usual," I said, looking hard at him.

Ruby widened her eyes and gave me a subtle shake of the head.

But Kenneth didn't seem bothered. "Is that right? Are you the high school type? On student council and all that? I'd believe it."

It was sneaky, the way he said it, but I knew it was a dig. "No," I said.

"Stella doesn't do extracurriculars," Ruby cut in. "She stays busy with AP classes. So how's the new game coming?"

"Great. I'm way ahead of deadline."

"What's it called?" I asked, thinking of the awful games I'd seen Marcus playing.

"Sorry, can't release that info. Competitors everywhere."

I glanced around at the fat-cat business population of South Bend. "Is it one of the really violent ones? Like with slo-mo of people getting blown up?"

"Don't tell me; you're a conscientious objector."

Ruby gave a nervous laugh. "Stel just can't handle blood and guts. She doesn't mean anything by it."

Kenneth sipped his drink. "It's human nature, sweetheart. Can't get away from it. People have been killing each other since the dawn of time. I'd say it's better on a screen than in real life."

"A lot of people say doing it on the screen leads to doing it in real life," I retorted. "What about Columbine?"

"Maybe those kids deserved to get shot. Don't tell me you

don't know some idiots that you wouldn't mind popping with a bullet or two." Kenneth gave a wicked grin as my jaw dropped.

"Kenneth, that's horrible. Sorry, Stella. He thinks it's funny to make people squirm," Ruby said.

"Squirm, squirm." I loaded as much irony as possible into my voice.

Kenneth chuckled. "You're quite a firecracker, aren't you? Somehow I'm guessing you're not going to design school like Ruby. What do you plan to study in college?"

I gave Ruby a swift glance, but she was careful not to meet my eyes. Design school! Talk about chameleon. "I'm not sure yet. Maybe social work, maybe history."

Kenneth waved his hand dismissively. "There's no money there. If you like history, you should get a business degree and then market yourself to companies as a researcher on historical trends in foreign markets. Did you know in Asia it's better to brand yourself as a company that's been around for a hundred years than it is to brand yourself as a new, cutting-edge company? It's their values. But without research, we wouldn't know that."

I stared at Kenneth coldly. "Maybe I'll stick to social work."

"You'll get tired of the hand-holding, believe me. Those people cry about not being able to pay their electric bill, then you do a family visit and find a big screen in the living room. I have a friend who's a public defender."

"It's nice that he respects the people he defends so much."

Ruby glanced between us, obviously anxious. Funny, I was feeling more comfortable around Kenneth than I thought I would. Maybe it was because I'd decided I hated him, and I didn't care what he thought.

"I don't think Stella likes me," Kenneth told Ruby, amused.

"No, she does! That's just how she is. Right, Stel?"

Poor Ruby. She was freaking out a bit, and I suddenly remembered what she'd said about wanting us to like each other. "That's right. I'm naturally antisocial," I agreed.

Kenneth laughed out loud. "Well, even if you don't like me, I like you. You have fire. I should have known Ruby wouldn't pick a wimpy friend." He wagged a finger at me. "Seriously, you should listen to me about the career thing. You're idealistic now, but money comes in handy later on. Say, for example, when you want to help someone quit smoking." His eyes rested on Ruby for a moment, and I wanted to slap him. I prayed that Ruby was too tipsy to realize he was making his point at her expense.

"Aw, you really believe she quit?" I couldn't help myself; it just came out, and too late I realized I had done the same thing he had.

Ruby looked back and forth between us. "Well, you're both being real jerks right now, aren't you?"

"I'm sorry," I said at the same time that Kenneth told her, "Relax, we were only kidding around. Waitress!" He beckoned a mousy girl in black slacks and a white shirt who was hurrying past, and she gave him a dirty look.

Thank goodness the real waitress appeared a moment later, and Kenneth ordered another round. Then he pressed some bills into her hand and said, "Hon, do you think you could convince Gregory to give us the VIP treatment? If he tells you no, go to Phil."

"What's the VIP treatment?" I asked when she walked away. Kenneth lifted his eyebrows. "Now, that would be telling."

By the time the waitress got back, I was burning with curiosity. She set down our drinks and said, "The treatment will be just a few more minutes." *The treatment?* I glanced around the lounge, trying to scope out hidden doors.

Kenneth watched me with a smile. He had moved closer to Ruby and was resting his Rolexed hand carelessly on her leg. I wanted to push it off. What was the matter with me? I knew they were together, so why was it killing me to see the evidence? Maybe because it was visually so wrong: the crow's feet when he smiled, his silver-streaked hair, and her meek as a freaking geisha—not the Ruby I knew at all. He definitely looked older than thirty-four.

At that moment our waitress reappeared, pushing a small dolly stacked with two steel boxes. Kenneth stood to let her access our seats.

"What are those?" I asked.

Ruby looked delighted. "I don't know. He's never done this before."

The waitress knelt and unloaded the boxes, setting one in front of Ruby and the other in front of me. "There are only the two," she told Kenneth apologetically. "You'll have to take turns."

"Don't worry about it, hon. It's more for them than for me."

The waitress unclasped the fastener on my box, spreading it open to reveal a metal basin. It was the shape of a large butterfly, and the bottom was coated in black, texturized rubber. She tilted her head up to look at me. "Heavy, medium, or light?"

"What?"

"Heavy, medium, or light pressure? Just take off your shoes and put your feet right in. Then I'll add the oil."

I swallowed a shocked laugh and eased off my pinching high heels. "Um, medium, I guess." I set my feet in the basin.

The waitress took a bottle of baby oil from her apron and squeezed in a generous amount, then fiddled with a switch on the side. I felt a sudden pulse of energy on the sole of each foot, then a steady pressure tracing my arch. As the rubber pads kneaded my feet, the waitress nestled a flannel cloth, something like a tea cozy, over the top of the machine. "It runs fifteen minutes. If you want to go again, just press the START switch."

I leaned back in my chair and marveled at the strange wonderfulness of a VIP foot rub machine. It felt fantastic, much better than those massage chairs in the mall.

Kenneth caught my eye and grinned. "Stick with me, and I'll take you places, little lady." His phony accent was so bad and the machines were so funny that I let out a snort of laughter before I could stop myself.

He nodded knowingly. "See? I'll win you over yet."

The smugness in Kenneth's voice sucked the laughter right out of me. I glanced at Ruby, who was busy arranging her feet in the basin, and gave him a cool stare. "No, you won't," I said loud enough for only him to hear.

Chapter Eighteen

The first few months of the new year slipped by peacefully, with no big assignments or tests. I think the teachers knew we needed a break after the pressure of college applications. But you know the saying: March comes in like a lion? This year it had new meaning for me.

I guess it was only a matter of time before the Ruby-Kenneth fiasco got out at school. South Bend was too small, and Ruby and Kenneth were too juicy.

I first got wind of it by a message from Tammy Nolan, my lab partner in biology. "Stella? This is Tammy. Call me. I heard the craziest thing about Ruby and this old man; and I mean, I know she's your . . . oh yeah, I keep forgetting you don't have your own voice mail." Then she said in a bright voice, "Hi, Stella's mom. Can you have Stella call me, please?"

I hit ERASE and called Tammy's cell right away. She was one of those girls who specialize in dish, and it was a bad sign if she knew about Kenneth. I barely managed hi before she launched in: "So, is it true? Bryce Leman saw Ruby and some, like, fifty-year-old guy at The South Bend Chocolate Company. She said he was playing with Ruby's hand, and he has *gray hair*."

I forced a laugh. "That is so ridiculous. Haven't you ever heard of early graying? Ruby's boyfriend is in his mid-twenties; he just has a few silver streaks."

"Oh. Just his mid-twenties? Are you sure? Bryce said he looked really old."

"Come on, you know Bryce. She exaggerates everything."

"Yeah, that's true. Well, everybody believes her about this one. It kind of sounds like something Ruby would do, you know?"

"Ruby can be a little crazy, but she wouldn't be into something sick like that."

"Are you sure?" Tammy didn't sound convinced. "You have to let me know if you find out something, okay? Call me whenever." I looked at the receiver in disbelief. *As if.* We chatted for a few more minutes before getting off the phone.

I poured myself a glass of iced tea and sat down at the kitchen table. Why was I even bothering with damage control? Ruby didn't care what people thought. But for some reason, I did.

School on Monday was not fun. People had always given Ruby looks, but now it was more obvious: the whispers, the stares, the glares. You'd think women would stick together instead of being so fast to hand out the scarlet letter. Why should they care if Ruby had an older boyfriend? But I knew the answer to

that: people can't stand someone who's different. Plus, Ruby
was too pretty. Of course they'd find a reason to hate her.

I did my best to circulate the "early graying" rumor, but
Bryce's story flew around a lot faster because people wanted
to believe it.

I was still stable old Stella, around since forever, so people
didn't sling me too much attitude; but I did catch some
walking around with Ruby. I was getting the weird sense that
people wanted me to pick, like there were sides: Ruby versus
everyone else. As the week wore on, the halls felt more and
more uncomfortable. Although Ruby barely seemed to notice.

Then Thursday came. Mrs. Leland was trying to get us
to understand the postmodern movement, and we were all
suffocating. As far as I could tell, postmodernists were the
most bored, beliefless bunch of people I'd ever heard of. That
thesis wasn't going to get me an A on the essay due in three
days, though, so I struggled to focus as Mrs. Leland read us a
poem about the death of truth.

From behind me Ruby gasped. I turned to look, and she
was staring at something in her notebook. Mrs. Leland finished
the poem and waited—one of her long, famous moments to
"let it sink in." Instead of the silence that usually happened,
Ruby demanded: "Who the hell went into my binder?"

Just like on that first day she'd come to our school, every
head whirled. I heard a few titters.

"Ruby . . ." Mrs. Leland looked nervous.

Ruby swiveled to face Rhetta, who stared right back at
her. "It was you, right? Next time why don't you grow some
balls and say it to my face?"

"Ruby, let's step outside for a moment." Mrs. Leland set a

hand on her shoulder, but Ruby twisted away.

"I'm done," she said.

"Are you sure?"

"Yes."

Rhetta muttered something under her breath, but Mrs. Leland flashed such a fierce look that even the principal would have quieted down. "Everyone, fifteen-minute free write, topic of your choice."

That was Mrs. Leland's method for settling the class when things weren't going smoothly. I pulled out a sheet of paper, scrawled, "What just happened?" and slipped it to Ruby when Mrs. Leland's back was turned.

In answer, Ruby removed a piece of paper from her binder and passed it back.

I spread it on my desk, sheltering it in the crook of my arm. It was a collage made of paper cutouts from various magazine ads. The centerpiece was the guy from the La-Z-Boy ad, a gray-haired old man leaning back in a recliner with a look of pure bliss. In the background were all kinds of money cutouts: pictures of cash, credit cards, and coins. In front of him, drawn in ballpoint pen, was a girl in a skimpy dress. Below her were the words: "How much is he paying you?"

I flushed. Those vindictive witches. Ruby had never done anything to them.

I shoved the collage into my binder and started to write a note. It was a little schizophrenic, a mix of comfort and outrage; but by the time the bell rang and we left together, Ruby didn't look as if she needed it.

"I can't believe they did that," I spit out.

Ruby shrugged. "I don't care about the collage. They're just pathetic bitches with nothing better to do. What bothers me is that someone went into my bag."

"Do you think it was Rhetta?"

"Well, it had to be someone in English, because I had my binder out in chemistry last period, and it wasn't there then. Also, I left my bag at my desk for a few minutes when I talked to Mrs. Leland about the essay. Rhetta was the only one sitting close enough to get to it. She hates me the most; and out of her, Stacy, and Lisa, she's the only one with the guts to stick it in there." Ruby ticked off the reasons on her fingers. "I bet they were all in on it, and they had a little arts and crafts night."

"Yeah, you're probably right," I agreed, feeling glum.

If Rhetta, Stacy, and Lisa were in on it, then so were the rest of the cheerleaders, and for that matter, half of the other cool people at Mishawaka High.

I had a flash of Colleen Carraway, a cute little blonde who'd moved to South Bend in fifth grade. She got a lot of attention from the boys, and it took the rest of us about two seconds to decide she was a slut. Rhetta and Kari Heilman led a pack of us girls from Mrs. McCrory's class to surround her at recess and ask, "Why are you such a slut?" and "Why do you pad your bra?" I remembered the righteous rage I'd felt toward Colleen, even though she hadn't done anything to deserve it. It's amazing the power of group-think.

"I'm going to nip this in the bud at lunch. I've had a bitch pack on my heels before; and if you don't stop it fast, it gets out of control." Ruby's voice was cold.

"At your old school in Utah?" I asked. Ruby never talked about friends from her past. Was that why?

She nodded but didn't say more.

❋

I sat through history and precalc, my brain snagging on Ruby's comment: *I'm going to nip this in the bud at lunch.* Knowing her, that could mean anything.

It was selfish and cowardly, but I didn't want to get caught in the cross fire. I'd been well liked for as long as I could remember, had never gotten involved in any stupid high school drama. I kept my hands off the guys that I knew other people liked, melted away when catfights started at parties.

But my neutral status was changing. My oldest friends wouldn't talk to me anymore, and since the Kenneth thing came out, people had been colder to me in general. Now Ruby was pulling on a T-shirt with a giant, painted-on target. She was like a match, bringing fire to everything she touched. I wasn't the one dating a senior citizen. This wasn't my battle.

I was all nerves at lunch, but Ruby was predictably chill. I attempted distraction: "You want to get a smoothie?"

"No, I have to handle Nakamura. Maybe tomorrow."

"What are you going to do?"

"I'll decide when I see her. Come on. You want to watch? It might be funny."

"Ruby, I don't know if you should."

Ruby gave me a look that shut me up better than any words could. "Where does she eat?" she demanded.

"The quad."

Ruby wheeled and headed in that direction. I sighed and followed her.

Every popular crowd naturally inherits the prime lunch spot, and other people just know to stay away. The picnic tables in the covered quad were like that. Emma Hausbeck, Stacy

Matthews, Lisa Holmes, Rhetta Nakamura, Luke Burrell, Brent Tano, Levi Hanks, and a bunch of their satellites were kicking back at the tables, eating and talking. Emma, always a show-off, had her shirt tied above her belly ring even though it was about five degrees out.

I saw the shift in attention as Ruby approached. It was like wind ruffling grass: heads turned, eyes followed her, and faces took on that gossipy look.

I hung back as Ruby walked to the table. Everyone fell silent, staring at her.

She said calmly, but loud enough for everyone to hear, "Rhetta, and whoever else put that note in my binder: if you try anything like that again, I'll make you sorry you ever met me. I have nothing to lose, and most of you do. So leave me the fuck alone." She surveyed the group, who stared at her wide-eyed, and then she pivoted and walked away.

The titters and whispers broke like a wave behind her.

"We're already sorry we met you," somebody called.

Emma Hausbeck lazily picked up a soda can, took aim, and pelted it at Ruby's back.

Ruby whirled around. Her face was pale. "Who did that?"

There were a few giggles.

"I said, Who did that?"

I wanted to blurt out "It was Emma!" but a primal instinct for self-preservation held me back.

"Do you really think anybody is going to tell you?" jeered Rhetta.

"Well, since you're all one pathetic organism, anyway, I guess it doesn't matter who it was." Ruby stepped forward and grabbed Lisa Holmes—probably the shyest and nicest of the cheerleaders—by the neck of her sweater. Lisa tried to jerk away, but Ruby was too fast: she threw a swift, hard punch that sent Lisa's head rocketing back like a doll with a broken neck. Blood gushed from Lisa's nose and spattered the ground.

Ruby stepped back, and Lisa crumpled into a squat, gasping for air.

There was a brief, intense silence, then somebody yelled, "Oh shit!"

Lisa's friends swarmed around her.

"Omigosh, are you okay?"

"I can't believe she punched you!"

"Lisa, can you say something?"

Lisa burst into tears.

"Here, use my sweatshirt."

"Hold her nose."

The yard monitor's whistle cut the air. She came pounding toward us, a heavy woman with short-cropped hair and a perpetual sheen of sweat on her face.

"She did it!" Emma shrieked, pointing at Ruby.

"I saw." The monitor spoke into her walkie-talkie and then said sharply to Ruby, "Stay right where you are."

Ruby shifted her weight to one hip and crossed her arms. Could she really be calm right now? I doubted it. I knew I should go over and ask if she was okay, but my limbs felt too frozen to move.

Mr. Montoya, Mrs. DeVries, and the school nurse were approaching at a fast pace. The nurse put an arm around Lisa as the administrators closed around Ruby like a circle of sharks.

"Show's over," Montoya called. "Everybody get out of here."

Reluctantly, the crowd dispersed. Montoya, our principal, had served ten years in the Chicago School District before coming to us, and we all knew better than to cross him. I tried to catch Ruby's eye, but she was zoning out as DeVries, the vice principal, read her the riot act in her whiny, aggressive voice.

I said a prayer for Ruby in my head as I escaped to class. The halls were already buzzing with gossip. I felt totally sick.

Chapter Nineteen

After school, as I was heading through the maze of people in the parking lot, I heard Tammy Nolan, my gossipy lab partner, call my name. I turned around, shading my eyes against the glare of the snow to find her as she cut through the crowd.

"I've been looking everywhere for you." Tammy caught up to me and clutched my arm. Her eyes were dancing. "Girl, everybody is talking. You know that thing at lunch? With Ruby?"

I stiffened. "Yeah?"

"Well, I just wanted to tell you: Rhetta and Emma and them are saying you must have known Ruby was going to do that. They said you didn't even ask if Lisa was okay; and if you're really going to pick Ruby over Lisa, then you better be ready to deal with the consequences."

"The consequences? What's that supposed to mean?" My voice was sarcastic; but it was only a mask for the scared, nauseous feeling I had inside.

"I don't know. They didn't say. But you know they're going to do something horrible to Ruby now," Tammy added with relish. "Why are you even friends with her? That was so messed up what she did to Lisa!"

"Yeah, but . . ." I didn't have it in me to tell the whole story: the collage, the soda can, the whole build-up. No, Ruby shouldn't have hit Lisa, but she had to do *something*. And if I had just opened my stupid mouth and told her it was Emma in the first place, she would have hit the right person.

Of course, then I would have been even more dead.

I felt a wave of resentment. Why did Ruby have to be so crazy and confrontational? Didn't she realize that her attitude affected other people, too?

Tammy misunderstood my silence. "I know, she probably gets you into college parties and stuff. But some things aren't worth it. No offense, but Rhetta could kick your ass. I'd watch my back if I were you."

"Thanks, Tammy," I said.

I climbed into my car and headed for Juniper Street. Ruby and I had to come up with a strategy. I wasn't sure if she would be home, but fighting almost always meant suspension.

Would this finally crack Gina's oblivion?

The roads were icy, so I had to drive like an old lady, which made me even more irritable. Finally I parked, ran up the steps, and knocked hard. Ruby played her iPod loud enough to drown out the whole world.

"Hold on!" Ruby hollered from somewhere inside. It felt like a long time before the door swung open. My eyes popped. She was wearing a peacock blue, floor-length dress with a deep slit in the leg. She struck a pose, hands on hips. "What do you think? Kenneth is taking me to *Madame Butterfly* in Chicago this weekend."

Suddenly I was so mad I could spit. Here I'd come over to help Ruby, and she clearly didn't have a care in the world. Maybe Tammy was right.

Ruby dropped the pose. "What's the matter?"

"Nothing. Nice dress."

"Seriously, what's the matter?"

"I said, nothing."

"Stel, don't pull that on me. That's a game to play with guys."

All at once I felt like crying. My feelings must have shown on my face because Ruby stepped forward and hugged me. She wasn't one for physical shows of affection, and it caught me off guard. "You freaked out about what happened today?"

"Yeah," I mumbled into her shoulder. "You're making it such a big thing that I have to choose sides."

"Nobody's making you do anything you don't want to do," Ruby said sharply, releasing me.

"No, but you're blowing this thing up so that somebody can't be friends with you and stay cool with everybody else."

"*I'm* blowing this thing up?"

"You punched somebody who didn't do anything, Ruby. That was kind of crazy." I couldn't stop the accusing, self-righteous tone in my voice.

She stared at me. "Is it really so important to you to 'stay cool' with everybody else?"

"Sorry if I don't want to be a social pariah for the rest of my senior year."

Ruby stepped closer until she was right in my face. "You

know what? You're an idiot if you buy into this high school crap. Every single one of those girls would turn on you on a dime. High school's almost over. It's not the real world. I'm doing what I have to do. But if you're scared it's going to rub off on you, then why don't you stay the hell away from me and go back to your real friends?"

The skin on my neck prickled as we stared at each other. I wanted to say something perfectly cold and brilliant to put her in her place, but humiliatingly, tears sprang into my eyes.

She was the only true friend I had left.

Ruby sighed. "I'm sorry. I didn't mean to be so harsh." She sank to her knees, sweeping the dress around her legs so that as little as possible was touching the porch, and patted the space next to her. I could have walked away right then, and it would have been a huge slap. But something made me sit down.

Ruby gazed out at the street for a minute before she started talking. "Look, I promised myself I wasn't going to talk about this ever again, but I'm going to tell you what happened at my old school in Utah. You have to promise never to bring it up again. And *don't* act all sympathetic."

I nodded, my anger slowing.

"So I lived in Utah for nine years, since third grade. I was part of the cool group, kind of like on a Rhetta or Emma level. There were four of us who were best friends: me, Jenny, Morgan, and Laila. Jenny and Morgan were Mormons, but they were cool Mormons. In tenth grade there was this guy, Jerod, who Morgan started to like. But he liked me. He was a total idiot, very frat boy, plus Morgan liked him, so when he asked me out, I said no. Well, he had a huge ego; he couldn't take rejection. It was so weird: I could tell he kind of hated me after that, but he kept going after me. It started to freak me out, because he'd hang around me at lunch and always sit by me at games and stuff. I started to feel like he was stalking me or something."

Ruby picked at a splinter of wood on the porch. "Anyway, I didn't know it, but he was talking all kinds of crap about me, about what a slut I was, and how I put out for him and a bunch of other guys, and how I was tempting Mormon guys on purpose. Morgan and Jenny and Laila started acting distant, but they wouldn't tell me why. Then there was this one night when we all went to a party at this guy Brett Farrell's house, and everybody got trashed. I mean, I drank almost a fifth of vodka by myself. Of course, I threw up, and then I went in this room to lie down for a while. Well, guess who found me there."

"Brett," I whispered.

"Yeah. He came in and lay down next to me, and I knew I should get up and leave, but I couldn't move. I was so wasted my limbs were, like, soggy, you know? I told him to get away from me, but he just laughed and put his hand on my leg. I tried to scream but he covered my mouth, and I knew I was going to get raped. Well, he got his fly down and he put himself between my legs, and this little voice in my head was screaming at my body to *do something.* I got this burst of adrenaline, and I bit his ear. He started yelling and trying to get away, but I kept biting down like a pit bull; you know, they don't let go until the other animal is dead. I bit part of his ear off."

I gasped.

"He ran out of there with his pants down and bleeding from his head, and everybody came running, and it turned into this whole crazy thing. He was saying I tried to get him to have sex with me, and when he wouldn't, I bit him; and I should be put in jail. Well, somebody called the cops, and I had to go down to the station all wasted. It was horrible."

"Did you tell them what happened? Did he get arrested?" I breathed.

"They didn't believe me. They said I didn't show any other signs of struggle. There was none of his skin under my fingernails or anything. I mean, I bit his *ear* off. Isn't that a 'sign of struggle'?"

"They believed *him*?" I asked incredulously. "They believed you were trying to seduce him and then just went crazy?"

"Yeah. I was trashed and he was sober. His dad was a judge on the district court and a bigwig in the Mormon church."

"That's *horrible.*"

"Yeah. Well, Gina talked to his parents, and they told her they wouldn't press charges if we didn't, and she agreed. She told me we wouldn't win the case anyway because of his legal connections, and it would only ruin the rest of my time in high school. I went along with it. That was the stupidest thing I ever did."

"I'm so sorry," I said again.

She gave me a fierce look. "I said no sympathy."

"Oh, sor—I mean, what happened after that?"

"I took a few weeks off from school because I was feeling kind of messed up, you know? When I went back, nobody would talk to me. Morgan and Jenny wouldn't even look at me. Laila told me that all the Mormon kids had been forbidden to associate with me; it had turned into, like, a churchwide thing. It was so insane. There was all kinds of clichéd stuff like people calling me names when my back was turned and messing with my locker, and I got pretty depressed. But I didn't want to let them beat me. I decided I was going to finish out the year no matter what, so I just ignored everything they did. Then this one day I was going down the steps after school, and somebody shoved me in the back so hard that I fell down the whole way and broke both wrists."

"Who was it?" I asked, shocked.

"I never found out for sure. As far as I'm concerned, it was all of them. That's when I told Gina we had to move or I was going to flip out and kill somebody. She said no. She cared more about her job than what was happening to me. That's the problem with her not being my real mom: when push comes to shove, she doesn't care that much."

I tensed. "What do you mean, she's not your real mom?"

Ruby sighed. "Gina is my dad's ex-wife. It's stupid Jerry Springer stuff. My dad was this corporate big shot; and he got some girl pregnant, and she wouldn't have an abortion. So she had the baby—that was me—and basically dumped me on him. You'd think it would be bad for his image, but Gina—she worked with him at the time but hadn't been with him yet— she says it was like, oh, look what a saint he is, raising this kid by himself. Well, that was crap. He definitely wasn't a saint. He had nannies watch me, and then he married Gina when I was four. They stayed married for a few years and then there was this scandal with him and this other woman, and he took off."

Ruby shrugged. "So Gina kept me. I was nine. She's been okay, actually. She lets me do what I want, and she pays for stuff. She's the only one that actually stuck with me, and we're not even related."

"That's crazy," I said. But it made sense. Everything was clicking into place.

"Yeah, well, don't bring that up again, either, okay?" Ruby gave me a quick glance.

"I promise," I said.

"Anyway, Gina said we couldn't leave Salt Lake because of her tenure track job, so I had to do something a little crazy so she would realize I was serious. Then she got the research position at Notre Dame, and we came here."

"What crazy thing did you do?"

"Lit the Mormon temple on fire."

That shocked me speechless. My head was whirling.

Ruby finally said, "I decided I would never, ever be part of a group like Morgan and Jenny and Laila again. I wasn't even going to talk to anybody here. But then that one day I really wanted a smoothie, and you ended up being okay."

We both laughed a little.

"I also decided I would never be passive again if somebody messed with me. It doesn't work. They feed on it."

I nodded, feeling like a complete idiot. My whole life, my religion had pounded in that I shouldn't judge anybody, and here I had done it to my best friend. "I'm sorry—" I started, but she hit my arm.

"Shut up. I *said* no sympathy."

"Oh, yeah."

We were quiet for a minute and then Ruby said, "Look, I get it if you don't want to screw up your senior year by being on the wrong side of those bitches. I know how bad it can be. We can just hang outside of school if you want."

I shook my head. "No."

Ruby looked at me to see if I was serious. And when she realized I was, a smile lit her face. But she didn't say anything. She just stood up and twirled. "Well? You never told me what you think about the dress. I'm going for forties' glam. Red lipstick, black eyeliner, lots of powder. Is it too over-the-top?"

"That depends. What shoes are you going to wear?"

"I'll show you." Ruby held the door open, and I followed her inside.

Chapter Twenty

Generally I like getting ready to go out, but Friday evening, preparing to meet Mike's parents, was like a new form of torture.

First my blush looked too heavy, then too light. My eyeliner wouldn't go on evenly. The only real leather shoes I had—and considering what I knew about Mike's parents, I wasn't about to wear any that weren't real leather—were two-inch brown heels, which didn't match ninety percent of the outfits in my wardrobe.

I finally picked a conservative brown dress with a simple V-neck and a calf-length skirt. I thought about wearing my fake pearls—they looked like the real thing to me—but I was sure Mike's mom would take one look and figure they came out of a Cracker Jack box. In the end I decided on no jewelry at all. At least I had a nice new purse.

Then, even though I slipped on my dress as carefully as if

it were made of glass, my deodorant left a streak halfway down the side. I scrubbed it and it finally disappeared; but when I used the blow dryer on the wet spot, it puckered the fabric. I prayed Mike's parents wouldn't notice, because I didn't have what it took to start over.

"Um, I didn't know you belonged to the Young Republicans Club," Jackie said when I emerged from the bathroom. "You look like an old lady gringa."

"That's better than a young slutty chola," I spat back.

"Marcus, doesn't she look like some old white lady going to bingo?" Jackie giggled.

Marcus, bless him, looked up from his bowl of Pepto-pink breakfast cereal and said, "No."

"Thank you, Marcus." I glared at Jackie and went back into the bathroom to obsess some more.

What seemed like two minutes later Marcus sang, "Your boyfriend is here!"

I rocketed out of the bathroom to beat Jackie to the door. I wanted to slip out before she could say something embarrassing. At least Mom was at work, so I didn't have to worry about her.

"Stel?" Jackie called from the couch as I was closing the door behind me. "You look pretty. I was just being a jerk."

I felt a rare flash of love for my sister. I stuck my head back in. "Thanks, Jackie." I pulled the door closed and turned to Mike.

He was looking very first-day-of-schoolish in pressed brown cords and a nice new parka, his cowlick tamed into submission. But it was more than his clothes; he had that nervy, spooked look a little kid gets before setting foot on the bus for the first time.

He kissed me on the cheek awkwardly. "Sorry I'm early. I'm kind of wired, and I couldn't sit around the dorm anymore." He looked at the door. "You want to hang out for a couple of minutes before we go? We still have half an hour before we're supposed to meet my parents at Tippecanoe."

"Okay, but let's stay out here. I know it's cold, but if we go in, Jackie and Marcus will be all over us."

"Sounds good to me." Mike pulled me into the wicker love seat on our porch and wrapped his arms around me. It felt good to cuddle with him before we had to face his parents. I needed to calm down, anyway: my pulse felt as if it had taken over my whole body.

Mike rested his chin on my hair. "My dad has already connected with half my professors to check up on me."

"Wow, that has to be annoying."

Mike sighed. "Yeah, he's a control freak. They can't wait to meet you, by the way. Dad keeps asking what you look like."

I snuck a glance at him. That sounded a little pervy, but I guess men were like that.

Mike was staring straight ahead with a funny expression on his face. "I hope you don't mind, but I said you were Spanish. My parents are a little . . . you know. And my mom went to Spain for an exchange program in college, so she loves anybody from there. If it comes up, could you go with it?"

It took a second to sink in. I stiffened in his arms. "You said I was *Spanish*?"

"Yeah." Mike sounded nervous. "They're a little . . . like I said. So is that okay?"

"No." I pulled away from him. "They're a little *what*? Racist?"

"No! Just old-fashioned."

"Then what's wrong with Mexican?"

"Nothing. But my dad grew up in a Boston Irish neighborhood. They had rivalries with the Mexicans and blacks and stuff."

I just stared at Mike.

Finally, he admitted, "Remember I told you about that girl Elaine? She was part black, and my dad freaked out. I really want them to like you."

My voice rose. "What is this, some weird rebellion? Your parents are racist, so you date minority chicks, but you don't have the guts to tell them?"

"That's a screwed-up thing to say!"

"It's screwed up to say I'm Spanish when I'm not."

Mike flushed. "I hate this PC crap where nobody can say anything anymore without being 'racist.' Look, based on a lot of people's preconceived notions, Spanish sounds classier than Mexican. So sue me."

I stood up. My legs were trembling. "Then maybe you should go find a Spanish girl to take to dinner with your parents, because I'm not going."

Mike looked alarmed. "Wait, you can't do that."

I snatched up my purse, the one I'd bought just to look nice for tonight. "Yes, I can."

"Stella, don't do this to me! I've been talking you up forever!"

I stared at him, equal parts shock and rage. I couldn't even get a curse word out. I walked inside and slammed the door behind me.

Jackie looked up, wide-eyed. "What happened?"

I stood at the door, seething. Would he have the nerve to knock?

I heard the love seat creak and then footsteps down the stairs. His engine started.

I thought I might combust. Marcus took one look and scurried past me to the den. But Jackie leaped off the couch.

"That asshole! What did he do?"

For some reason that did it. My eyes filled with tears.

Jackie slid a bony arm around my shoulders and pulled me toward the couch. She was so skinny—shooting up so fast. "Guys are all the same. Don't let it get to you."

Surprisingly, this piece of thirteen-year-old wisdom was comforting. I let her push me into a seat. "Yeah, maybe you're right."

"I'm definitely right. Stay there and I'll make us popcorn and you can tell me what happened." Popcorn was our family cure-all, the thing Mom made when we were sick, sad, or bored.

"I can't eat right now. I'm too mad," I told her. When she didn't stop moving toward the kitchen, I said, "Extra salt." It occurred to me that Jackie had the makings of a good girl friend; maybe after ten years or so, when the age gap didn't matter as much, we could be tight.

I heard the microwave open, and the soft explosion of kernels, and water running into a pan. I was still in shock. *Did Mike really do that?* Nobody had ever made me feel bad—I mean *really* bad—about being Mexican before.

A few minutes later Jackie came out loaded with a bag of extra buttery popcorn and two mugs of cocoa. There were so many melted marshmallows that my chocolate looked like a cappuccino overflowing with foam.

I accepted a cup and clutched it to my chest. Jackie fussed with the throw pillows, ripped open the popcorn bag, and generally got things just right. Then: "Did he dump you?" she demanded.

"No." I glanced at her, weighing how much to tell her. I had never confided in Jackie before. She was a kid. But she looked so eager, and the chocolate and popcorn were so sweet. I sighed and told her what happened.

Jackie was a pretty good listener, it turned out. She didn't interrupt, like Christine would; and she didn't give too much advice, like Mom would. She was more like Beth, saying "Uh-huh" and "Yeah" and "What a jerk" at the right moments and letting me get through my story.

When I was done, she said, as if it were the most obvious thing in the world, "Well, he's a racist ass, and you should dump him."

But already I was questioning my own judgment. "Are you sure? Because I don't think he's racist exactly; I mean, he's in a relationship with me, so how could he be? It's his parents who are racist. He just cares too much about impressing them."

Jackie gave me a withering look. "*A*: He can totally be in a relationship with you and still be a racist; look at Thomas Jefferson, Columbus, and like a million random slave owners; *B*: he's not only a racist, he's a *wussy* racist."

I smiled. "Yeah, okay." I didn't want to talk about it anymore, though. I needed some time to process. I still wasn't sure if Jackie was missing the layers of complexity in the situation or if she had hit on the truth.

"So what's up with you? Are you and DaShawn turning

into a thing?" I asked. It was to change the subject, but also because I needed to know.

I hadn't seen DaShawn at our house again, but I'd heard from Tammy Nolan that he and Jackie were hanging out a lot at Rick's Pool Hall. As far as I was concerned, DaShawn had a whole forest of red flags sprouting from that pocket where he tucked the red bandanna.

Jackie shook her head. "Nah, we're tight, but not like that."

I didn't believe her for a second. DaShawn would never let a girl as hot as Jackie slide by as a friend. "Just please don't sleep with him. He could write a manual on how to be a player." I was trying for light, but it didn't come out that way.

Jackie stared at me. "Did you not hear what I said two seconds ago? We're just friends."

"Whatever you say. But I don't trust him, okay? I don't want him to hurt you."

"No, you don't trust *me*," Jackie said bitterly. She got up and walked out of the room.

I watched her go in her too-tight jeans, with her perfect rear and her long black hair, and I realized it was true. I *didn't* trust her. I mean, I knew about her grades and test scores and big old brain, but I still couldn't get past the chola-slut wrapping. To me, it was what failure looked like for a Mexican female.

Mike's words jumped into my head: *Look, based on a lot of people's preconceived notions, Spanish sounds classier than Mexican. So sue me.*

And I knew what he meant. I wondered if that made me racist, too.

Chapter Twenty-one

It's funny how you can wake up in the morning and think everything is okay for a few seconds before reality comes crashing down. It was like that Saturday: Mom woke me up with a foot rub, our weekend tradition, and I came to in a groggy state of bliss.

Then Mom asked, "So how did it go last night?"

"Hmmm," I muttered, pretending to be too asleep to answer; but the question was like a punch.

Mom gave my foot a final squeeze. "You can tell me later. I have to get ready for work." She left the room, and I gazed blearily at my clock. Ten-thirty.

The phone hadn't rung since I'd gotten home last night. But Mike probably wasn't even up yet, I rationalized. Then I caught myself and thought furiously that I shouldn't care whether he called; he'd gone too far, and things were over.

Thank God I hadn't slept with him.

But we had done more than we probably should have. I missed him with irrational parts of me. My heart and body, when they ganged up, were much louder than my brain.

I eyed the cordless lying on my bedside table. I needed Ruby's advice. But, of course, she wouldn't answer. Ruby didn't answer before noon on weekends *ever*. I could picture her curled up in a nest of comforters, hair in a funny bun on top of her head, sock draped over her eyes, snoring lightly. I called her just in case, but hung up when her voice mail clicked on.

Beth. My fingers danced over the familiar numbers on the keypad, but I stopped short of dialing the last digit. She didn't want to talk to me; she'd made that clear.

Yes, she does, whispered my rational self. *Beth and Christine love you; they just think* you *don't love* them.

But I still couldn't bring myself to dial. Pride is a funny thing. Even when you know it's causing you problems, it sits there like a block in your chest and refuses to let you take action.

Irritated, I got out of bed and rummaged through my closet for some running shorts. I needed to pound out some stress. I dreaded the breakfast table with Mom's innocent questions. Also, the fact that Jackie knew everything seemed crazy in the light of day. What had I been thinking? As if she could possibly relate.

Running outside in South Bend in the early spring was like a suicide mission. The snow was starting to soften, and in some areas turning to slush; but there were still patches of old ice on the sidewalks. When I'd fallen twice, once on each knee, I started running on the edge of people's lawns, crunching through crisp grass. I did a loop across the river that way, thinking about Mike the whole time.

What if I'd been too hard on him? I always broke up with guys. This was the longest relationship I'd had—six months—and I'd be throwing it all away if I just gave up now.

By the time I got back I was frostbitten, limping, and insecure about how I'd acted the night before.

I pushed through the front door to find Jackie with a plate of toaster waffles balanced on her lap, flipping through a textbook. "The Ku Klux Klan called," she said.

"You are *so* funny. When?"

Jackie's eyes flicked up. "Does it matter? You're not calling him back, are you?"

"Is that any of your business?"

"Hypothetically, what would be going too far? Calling you a Spic to your face? Asking you to mow his lawn?"

"Shut up. This is totally different."

Jackie lifted her eyebrows in reply.

I stormed to my room. Why had I told her anything? Stupid, stupid, stupid.

The cordless was in the hall, and I hesitated a moment before picking it up. I wanted to call Mike back so badly my fingers ached. I felt schizophrenic: mad but needy, hurt but unsure if I had a right to be. I needed more time to think. I decided not to call him; he would have to call me again.

He would have to work for it.

That resolution lasted for about half an hour. During that time I wandered back and forth to the kitchen, polishing off a whole box of Pop-Tarts. When I considered opening a second box—cinnamon flavored, not even my favorite—I knew things were getting out of hand.

I muttered "Bastard," and dialed Mike's number.

Mike sounded happy, breezy even, when he answered. "I'm so glad you called. I was starting to worry. We have to talk. What are you doing right now?"

"Nothing."

"Can I come get you?"

"Um . . ."

"Please?"

The sweet, pleading tone in his voice did me in. "Okay."

"Great. I'll pick you up in half an hour."

As soon as I hung up, I felt like I'd been bamboozled. By myself, no less.

I flew into the shower and then tore through my closet, feeling panicky. So much for self-control. I was like those pathetic girls who whine about their cheating, beating boyfriends and then jump back into their arms when they show up with a box of Russell Stover.

I flung my favorite jeans and camel sweater—an outfit that Ruby had started calling "Old Faithful"—on the bed, and began to sift through the pile on my closet floor for my boots.

"Where are you going?"

I wheeled around to find Jackie leaning on my door frame, eyeing the outfit I'd laid out. "None of your business."

She clapped the edge of her hand to her forehead. "Tell Mike I said '*Sieg Heil*.'"

"Those were Jews, not Mexicans, you idiot."

"Same difference to a racist." Jackie disappeared down the hall. I thought of throwing something after her, but I was down to ten minutes. Mike was never late.

I yanked on my clothes, pulled a brush through my hair, and was furiously dotting on concealer when the doorbell rang. I snatched my purse and raced downstairs.

Mike was holding a bouquet of Gerbera daisies. My first thought was: *Those are the cheapest kind,* but I accepted them sweetly, praying that Jackie wouldn't get any bright ideas to come downstairs and mouth off.

While I put them in a vase, Mike waited for me on the couch, leafing through a newspaper. It bothered me that he looked so relaxed. A little anxiety would have been nice. Or, to be honest, tearstains and him on his knees.

When we got to his car, Mike held open the door for me, something he hadn't done since our first couple of dates.

"Where are we going?" I asked coldly.

"Somewhere private. After that we can go to Lula's and I'll buy you lunch, if you still feel like talking to me." Mike gave me his most charming smile.

He drove a few blocks up the road, then parked at the entrance to the middle school playfield. It was empty at this time of year, covered in a blanket of footprints and dirty snow. The whole neighborhood let their dogs run loose there, and little kids often tried snowshoeing. It wasn't exactly the most romantic setting.

Mike cut the motor and turned to face me. "I really messed up. You were right when you said I care too much about what my parents think. My dad's a little racist, and I didn't want to admit that to you or deal with what he'd say if he knew you were Mexican, so I took the easy way out. I've been feeling really bad about it. I'm sorry."

I stared at him. He sounded totally rehearsed.

"Stella?"

"What?" I snapped.

"Did you hear what I said?"

"Yeah."

Mike took my hand. "I think I love you. Can you forgive me?"

I blinked. He'd said the *L* word. But *I think?*

Mike must have seen something on my face, because he quickly said, "I mean, I do love you. Can we just start over?" His face was earnest now, and I was reminded of what Ruby had said a while ago: men truly want nothing more in the world than to win you. Then when they have you, they come back down to earth.

"I don't know," I said.

Mike looked shocked—finally some real emotion. "You won't give me another chance?"

Six months of togetherness pulled at me hard. The familiarity of his smell, his warm arms, the athletic muscles in his back and chest and legs. It was all the physical stuff calling me, and I thought vaguely that we really are hardwired to mate for life.

"Okay," I said slowly. "But you have to tell your parents the truth. That I'm not Spanish."

There was a silence. Mike's hold loosened on my hand. Finally he said, "Okay. I'll tell them."

I should have fallen into his arms. It should have felt like a victory for both of us. Instead, it felt like a lukewarm truce.

Mike leaned forward and kissed me tentatively. "So you forgive me?"

"Yeah." But I could hear the resentment in my voice. Things still weren't right. I squeezed Mike's hand. "Just tell your parents, okay?"

He gave me a look and pulled back to start the car. "Yeah, I know. You already said that. You don't want me to do it this second, do you?"

I stared out the window. "I guess not. What reason did you give for me not being there last night?"

"I said you were sick. Are you going to make me tell them the truth about that, too?" Mike's voice held a hint of sarcasm.

"No."

"Sorry," he said, his voice softening. "It was probably too soon to ask you to meet them, anyway. I know it was a lot of pressure. Let's just try to go back to where we were before they came, okay?"

"Okay," I said.

"You still up for Lula's?"

"I guess," I told him. I felt bizarrely like I was losing.

Chapter Twenty-two

I felt disoriented the next week. Everything was back to "normal," except really it wasn't. Mike and I saw each other almost every day, as if we were trying to prove that everything was fine; I checked the mail obsessively for Notre Dame envelopes; and Rhetta, Emma, and the others left Ruby and me alone. But I should have known something bad was coming.

I walked out of Mike's dorm on Thursday after a couple of hours cuddled up watching sports. It was snowing lightly, and already the dirty, rutted snow on the ground was taking on a fresh sparkle. I picked my way through the drifts in the visitor lot—the plowers were lazy and scraped each new layer of snow into the same frozen heap—and brushed my windshield free of flakes. The last bit of sun was illuminating the horizon, though it was only 5 p.m. I wanted to get home because Mom had a rare night off and had promised us homemade lasagna.

When I pushed open the door to my house, I brought in a flurry of snow with me. The lights were dim, and at first I thought Mom and Jackie were cuddled up on the couch.

"Honey, I'm home," I hollered.

There was a sniff, then "Hey, Stel." It was Ruby in Mom's arms. Mom glanced up and shook her head slightly.

I closed the door, dropped my bag, and hurried to the couch. Ruby pulled away from Mom and tried to smile at me. Her eyes were swollen and red. I sat next to her, sure that Kenneth had done something awful. "What happened?"

Ruby mumbled something and began to breathe fast, like she was going to cry. Mom tried to pull her close again, but Ruby shook her head and pressed her palms against her eyes. "No, I'm okay. Just give me a second."

Mom stood. "I think we need popcorn. And tea with milk and sugar. I'll be back in a few minutes."

I scooted closer to Ruby, noticing the sour smell of alcohol. I didn't dare try to hug her.

"Get out my phone. It's in the front pocket of my bag." Ruby wiped her nose fiercely on her sleeve.

I pulled out her bag from under the coffee table and found the phone. Without a word, Ruby opened her e-mail, scrolled down, and clicked on an attachment.

At first I couldn't tell what it was; it came through too big for the small screen of her phone. But then the image adjusted, and I gasped. There was a photo of Ruby's face spliced onto some awful piece of Internet porn: a naked woman posing in an attempt to be sexy. She was clearly an amateur: her breasts sagged, her belly revealed the thin scar of a C-section, and patches of cellulite shadowed her thighs and stomach. She wore two black garters and a funny leather belt. It was pathetic.

But worse, it was convincing.

Whoever did this was really good at Photoshop. The woman's body wasn't fat; it was soft and disproportionate. Ruby's head melted flawlessly into the woman's neck. It was believable—for someone who hadn't seen Ruby naked—that this might really be how she looked under her clothes.

The subject line read: "For a good time, call Ruby Caroline"—and then her phone number.

I had no words.

"They e-mailed it to Gina. It's probably all over the web by now."

"Where did they get the picture of your face?" I asked.

"It's my yearbook picture. The one we had to take last month."

I sucked in my breath. Emma's boyfriend, Luke Burrell, was on the Yearbook Committee. He would have access to all the photos in the database.

"We have to go to the police," I said.

Ruby gave me a warning look. My mom was emerging from the kitchen, holding a tray with steaming mugs and a bag of popcorn.

I slid Ruby's phone back into her bag. Mom raised her eyebrows but didn't mention it. "I added the milk, but I'll let you girls put in the sugar. I don't know how sweet you like it."

Ruby accepted the hot mug and leaned back, cradling it close to her chest. "Sorry I freaked out, Mrs. Chavez. There are just some bitches at school."

Mom didn't blink at the language. She patted Ruby's leg and said, "High school girls can be awful. Is there anything I can do to help?"

"Can Stella spend the night at my house?"

Mom nodded. "Absolutely."

We were all quiet for a while, sipping our tea. Then Ruby blurted out, "Also, will you pray for me?"

Mom's face was tender. "Of course I will. I already do. And you can pray, too, you know, honey."

Ruby made a noncommittal sound and looked away. Neither Mom nor I were about to interrupt whatever was going on in her head. Sounds of Marcus's video game drifted from the den and filled the silence. Finally Ruby set down her cup, still mostly full, and said, "You want to head to my house now, Stel?"

I nodded and started clearing up our mugs and snack. Mom stayed on the couch, watching us. I remembered then that she was going to cook lasagna. When Ruby took her plate to the kitchen, I whispered, "I don't want to miss your night off. Should I ask her to stay to dinner?"

Mom shook her head. "Go. She needs you right now."

Our eyes met in understanding.

I figured that once Ruby and I were in the car we'd be able to talk, but if anything I felt even more awkward. Ruby was limp against the seat, blank and tired looking. Anything I thought to say seemed inadequate.

"Sometimes I understand those kids at Columbine," Ruby said suddenly. "Did you ever think about killing anybody? . . . Never mind. Of course you haven't. You're perfect."

I surprised myself by what I admitted next. "Yes, I have."

Ruby looked at me.

"For years I used to think about killing my dad. I was just a kid. These images would come into my head: me looking right in his eyes and stabbing him with a knife."

"Do you really think you'd do it if you had the chance?"

"Of course not," I said. "Hey, don't you go and do something insane. If I have to burn up my savings to bail you out of jail, I'll kill *you*."

It was a joke, but neither one of us laughed.

"I need to get really, really high," Ruby said abruptly. "Is there anywhere you can score on the street in South Bend?"

"Score what? Weed?"

"No. Not coke, either. Something I've never tried before."

"Does such a thing exist?"

"Junk, Special K, angel dust, 2C-B . . ."

I cut her off. "First of all, I have no idea what half that stuff is. And second of all, I have even less idea where we'd get some."

Ruby gestured impatiently. "Just drive to the worst part of town. I'll figure it out from there."

I frowned. How many drugs did Ruby and Kenneth do, anyway? It hit me that it had taken Mom years to figure out that Dad was an addict, and she was married to him. "Are you nuts?"

"Maybe."

"I don't know, Ruby," I said. I glanced over at her to gauge her reaction.

Tears were pooling in her eyes. She looked like she might be on the edge of a breakdown.

I considered. It was still early evening. There were definitely some shady parts of town, but nowhere actually dangerous to drive, like you'd find in Chicago. The snow was coming down so hard I doubted anyone would be out. No dealers, for sure. South Bend didn't operate like that.

What if I just took a quick detour to make her feel better? We'd drive through fast, and maybe she'd calm down and forget about finding drugs once she realized no one was around. "How about that area by South Street? That's kind of ghetto."

"That's good."

"One drive through the main part, then we go home. If you don't see anybody, you don't see anybody."

"That's fine," Ruby agreed.

We drove through the quiet streets, flakes swirling against the windshield. As we got farther south, neat storefronts gave way to mini-marts with barred windows, pubs in tin shacks, and adult video stores. The sidewalks were abandoned, snow piling up quickly.

"Pull over," Ruby demanded.

"Why?" I was already slowing for a red light.

"I want to talk to those kids back there."

I looked in the rearview, and sure enough, there were a couple of junior high–aged kids plodding along, heads down against the weather. They were both in oversize parkas, lugging backpacks. The snow almost hid them from sight. "Ruby, they're like thirteen. They're not going to sell you anything."

"Thirteen-year-olds always know where the drugs are." Ruby hopped out of the car as the light flicked to green.

I had no choice but to cross and pull over to the side, motor idling. I followed her in my rearview mirror with anxious eyes as she strode down the sidewalk. At least they were just kids,

I thought, not old enough to be a threat to a crazy chick like Ruby . . . I hoped.

Ruby stopped the kids, and they talked for a few moments in a huddle. When one of them pointed down a side street, I felt a stab of worry.

Ruby turned and trotted back to the car, letting in a gust of cold air as she climbed inside. She was grinning, cheeks stung red by the wind. "Bingo. Two blocks down that street, the blue house with the bashed-in mailbox."

"No," I said. "No way."

"You knew what we were coming here for!"

"I told you I would drive you down the main street so if you saw a kid selling, you could buy some. I am *not* going to some dealer's house. Do you want to get killed?"

"I don't care."

"Well, I value my life. Let's go home. Call Kenneth and he'll bring you something."

"Fine, I'll go by myself." Ruby pushed open the door and got out again.

"Ruby!"

She waved at me. "Go on. I won't hold it against you. I know I'm being insane."

"No! I'm not leaving you! Get in the car!"

"Sorry!" She slammed the door with a huge smile. The lunatic, she was enjoying this.

Fine, let her get killed, I thought. I peeled forward, wheels skidding, and flipped a U at the next light in time to see her disappear around the corner. She was really going to do this.

I pulled to the side of the road and slammed the steering wheel in frustration. I couldn't just leave her. I didn't have a cell; and even if I did, who would I call? The police? My mom? Besides, someone might not get there fast enough to stop something bad from happening. Women were way more likely to get raped if they were alone, I'd read.

I swore and hit the gas, making a sharp turn onto the street. I caught up with Ruby and rolled down the window. "Ruby, please. I can't leave you. Can you please get in the car?"

"No. Just go home, Stel. I'm a big girl."

"Yeah, well, full-grown women get raped every day," I said.

"I might like it."

I wanted to shake her.

I rolled up the window and drove down the next block, to the house with a bashed-in mailbox. Ruby didn't look surprised to see me leaning against the car waiting for her, scarf pulled over my head like a hood. "I told you to go home," she said.

I shook my head. "I'm coming with you. But I'm never going to forgive you for this. This is fucking stupid, and you're putting both our lives at risk."

"*I'm* putting *my* life at risk. *You're* putting *your* life at risk. Capisce?"

I was too mad to answer. I just followed her up the steps and prayed that no one would be home.

The bell echoed inside the house, and a chorus of vicious barks broke out. Nails skidded on hard flooring, and paws thumped against the door.

"Lacy! Tito! Get down!" There was a heavy thud and a whine. I shrank back, ready to run. Something clicked, and the door opened a crack. "What do you want?"

I couldn't see anything but a thin slice of face and a suspicious eye. "I want to talk to Nick or Jason," said Ruby.

"Shanae Bryant said we could find them here."

The door opened farther to reveal a thin, olive-skinned man with a long black ponytail and a goatee. He had close-set eyes and a twisted mouth—a scar? He was wrapped in a pale blue terrycloth bathrobe. On anyone else, it would have looked silly; but I didn't have the slightest desire to laugh. "Shanae? Isn't that Terrell's kid?"

Ruby nodded.

"I'm Nick. What do you want?"

Ruby leaned forward and whispered something.

Nick frowned. "I don't know what you're talking about." He started to shut the door.

So fast it seemed like magic, Ruby whipped out money from her pocket. She cradled it in her hand so he could see the thickness of the roll. "I got a lot more where this came from. You don't want to sell to me, fine, you'll never see me again. But you give me some good stuff, and you've got a new customer."

I stood there, completely nauseous.

Nick's eyes lingered on the roll. "How much you got?"

"Four hundred bucks. I'll buy two-hundred worth of something, and you can keep the other two hundred for a tip."

"Hold on." The door shut in our faces. "Jason!" Nick yelled from inside. His footsteps receded.

Ruby and I looked at each other. I shoved my hands into my pockets. I'd been gripping the icy railing, and my palm was frozen. Ruby tucked her money back into her pocket and lifted her eyebrows at me as if to say *So far, so good.* I glared at her.

A few minutes later the door opened again. A short, stocky man with a crew cut surveyed us. He looked about thirty, and his eyes were a cold, bright blue. He wore an old IUSB sweatshirt and jeans. He shifted his weight, considering us, I guess. Finally, he opened the door farther and stepped back to let us in.

Ruby walked inside without hesitating. I went, too, though every instinct in my body was screaming to turn around.

A low, menacing growl cut the air; but the man said "Tito," and the growl turned into a whine. Tito crouched and thumped his tail on the floor. He was a Rottweiler, not much older than a puppy, with powerful muscles bunched under a shiny black and rust coat. The other dog, a bigger Rottweiler, stared at us. Her lips were pulled back just enough to show she was ready to attack, but she made no sound or movement.

The man immediately closed the door behind us and slid a bolt and chain into place.

I tried to breathe normally.

"You're Jason?" asked Ruby.

The man nodded. The room we were in was dark and cramped, with too much furniture. Afghans were draped over everything, and thick curtains hid the windows. A pizza box lay open on the glass coffee table, revealing crusts and strands of old cheese. The air smelled like stale cigarettes.

Jason's eyes flicked over Ruby and me. The skin on his face was pitted with acne scars. He stepped toward me. "I'm going to pat you down." He swiftly patted my body, feeling between my thighs, up and down my legs, even over my socks. "Take off your jacket."

I stared at him blankly.

"I said, take off your jacket."

"Stella, do what he says," Ruby hissed.

I shrugged off my parka.

"I'm going under your shirt to look for wires. Stand still."

I stared straight ahead as his fingers traveled my stomach, my back, and my breasts. He was as quick and methodical as a doctor, but I still felt a hot flush of shame.

"I want to do the other one." Nick spoke from the back of the room, where he was leaning on the arm of a couch, watching with obvious enjoyment. "She got nice tits."

"Shut up." Jason moved to Ruby. He was equally quick with her. When he finished, he leaned close and whispered something in her ear. She looked alarmed, and I felt my stomach twist in fear.

But Jason stepped back and said, "Okay, what are you looking for?"

"What do you have?" asked Ruby.

"I said, what are you looking for?"

"I don't care. Not coke or weed. I have four hundred dollars. I'll buy something for two hundred, and you can keep the other two since it's our first deal." Ruby jerked her head toward Nick. "That's what I told him."

Jason nodded. "Let me see the money."

Ruby dug into her pocket and handed him the roll of bills. He flipped through it quickly, then tucked it away. "Nick, get a couple bags of smack. I want to keep an eye on these two."

Smack? I cast an anguished glance at Ruby, but she was watching the man. "I don't have any needles. I never tried smack before."

He allowed a small, cold smile. "You'll like it. Everyone does. You don't need needles, you know. Just put it on foil, light underneath, and inhale the smoke. You want to take a hit before you leave? I'll show you."

"No," I said.

Both of them glanced at me in surprise.

Ruby seemed about to argue, but then she must've thought better of it. "Okay. I guess she's right. We have to go."

"You sure?" There was something in Jason's tone that I didn't like.

"Maybe some other time."

Jason's eyes narrowed. "I'm doing you a favor, here. Maybe you should *make* time."

Ruby glanced at me. I saw that, finally, she was nervous, too. "I think . . . we really have to go. People are going to wonder where we are."

"Who knows you're here?"

"Nobody!" Ruby assured him.

One corner of Jason's mouth lifted into an ironic smile. A creak sounded somewhere and I jerked around, sure it was another man who'd take us to a back room, get us wasted on heroin, and rape us with Jason and Nick.

A small face peered in from the doorway of the hall. "Dad?" All I saw were enormous eyes, lost under a fringe of black hair, and pale skin.

Jason frowned. "How many times I told you to stay in your room when I got company?"

Was it a girl or a boy? Eight? Nine years old? The eyes widened. "But *Dad*, I'm hungry."

"Get in your room, Macy. You can eat later."

"But I'm hungry *now*." With an accusing glare at us, Macy turned and shuffled back down the hall.

Almost at the same moment, Nick emerged from a doorway on the opposite side of the room clutching a brown paper bag. He glanced at Jason, who gave a quick nod. Nick opened the bag and allowed Ruby to peer in as Jason unbolted the door.

"I'm walking them out. Bring it when I call," Jason instructed Nick. He stood aside to let us out first and then scanned the street as he escorted us to the car, his whole body tense. He peered through the car windows, right hand gripping something inside his pocket. A gun?

"Unlock it and pop the trunk," Jason ordered.

He sifted through the mess of wrappers in the backseat and the library books and binders and soccer gear filling the trunk. Finally he took out his cell and made the call. A moment later Nick darted across the street, barefoot. He shoved the bag at Ruby, dancing in the snow.

Jason looked hard at Ruby. "Don't send anyone to us, you understand? And don't show up again. You need something, you call the number in the bag." He stepped back and allowed us into the car.

I had trouble fitting the key into the ignition, and I realized my hands were shaking. Finally the engine caught and I pulled forward. Nick had already run back across the street and into the house, but Jason stood and watched as we drove away, arms folded against his chest.

"We pulled it off," Ruby breathed as we turned off the street.

I blinked, holding back tears.

"Stella, don't. It's okay. We're fine. That went perfect!"

I slammed my hand on the wheel. "It did not go perfect!"

She stared at me in shock.

I stepped on the gas and drove fast, trying to get out of this horrible little neighborhood, which I swore I'd never visit again as long as I lived.

"I'm sorry. I didn't know you'd freak out this bad," Ruby finally ventured.

I pulled over to the side of the road, skidding on the fresh snow, and grabbed the bag from her lap. I opened my door and threw it into the middle of the street. Before Ruby could react, I slammed the door shut and hit the gas.

It took a moment to sink in. Then she freaked. "What the hell did you do that for? Stop the car! Let me out!"

"No."

"Let me out *now*," she growled.

I sped up.

"That was four hundred bucks! And I just went through that for nothing? So you could pitch a fit? You're a real friend!" Ruby's voice was dangerously high.

"You don't know anything about friendship, Ruby," I spat out. "You don't know that I had no other choice except to go in there with you. *You* put me in that position. You also don't know that I'm a real friend for throwing that stuff away, because smack will *kill* you. As in dead and gone forever. God, you're stupid. And you're selfish."

"Take me home."

"Don't worry. I will."

We drove the rest of the way to Ruby's house in silence. I pulled into her driveway, and she got out and slammed the door without a word.

I felt nothing. Not angry, not sad. Just numb.

After dropping off Ruby, I drove to the mini-mart down the street from her house. I scooped some change from the bottom of my purse and fought through the wind and snow to the pay phone. A tattered old phone book clung to the fixture by a metal coil. I flipped through. Half the pages were missing or torn, but I found the nonemergency police number inside the front cover.

A female dispatch answered.

"I need to report that a bag of heroin was thrown out of a car on South Street at about Thirty-fifth. It's in the middle of the road right now, if somebody hasn't taken it."

"Name, please?" The woman sounded bored. She must get crazy calls like this every day.

"Just pick it up, okay? I don't want some little kid getting it." I placed the receiver on its cradle and plodded back to my car.

All I wanted was my bed.

The streets were abandoned as I drove home. It was turning into a regular spring blizzard.

Chapter Twenty-three

Friday I decided to skip school. It wasn't something I normally did, but I needed *not* to see Ruby or deal with schoolwork or listen to one more person talk about the porn picture of Ruby or the billion schools they had applied to.

I spent the morning frittering away: long bath, lots of tea, the second half of *The Great Gatsby*. My mom would be finished with her shift by two, so at noon I finally got dressed and started thinking about what to do with the rest of the afternoon. If I was going to give this thing with Mike another chance, I needed to spend more time with him.

He sounded excited to hear from me. "Come over! I don't have class until five, and Kamal's not here. We can chill."

I knew what "chill" meant, and lately I hadn't wanted to. Something had been missing since the big fight. "How about we get a bite to eat at the Chocolate Company? Or we could get sandwiches at Enrico's."

"Are you hungry?"

"No, that's why I said we should get food."

"You are *so* funny. Okay, meet me at the deli in half an hour. We can go back to my room after."

I made a noncommittal sound.

I was a couple of minutes late to meet Mike. The plows had been slow, so traffic was congested even though it was early afternoon. I finally found a parking spot and hurried to meet him inside our favorite deli, an Italian place with red-checked tablecloths and Frank Sinatra–type music on the crackling loudspeakers. The food was to die for: big rounds of salami and fresh sausage and prosciutto behind a glass case, creamy balls of mozzarella floating in tubs of water, basins of olives soaking in brine. The owner would cut whatever you wanted into thick slices and pile it on baguettes with plenty of butter. Weird, I know, but apparently the way Italians like it.

When I walked in, Mike was already sitting down, staring at his phone with such focus that he didn't even notice my arrival. I cleared my throat theatrically, and he jumped. "Stella! I didn't hear you come in."

"Did I scare you?"

"No."

I smirked. "Yeah, right." I pulled out the chair opposite him and sat down.

"Look at this." He showed me his phone. The screen showed a thumbnail of the Ruby picture. "Is she seriously hooking?"

I glanced at it and looked away, not wanting to see the awful image again. "Of course not. There are just some evil girls at school who don't like her. They doctored it in Photoshop."

"It doesn't look doctored."

"Yeah, they're good."

Mike let out a low whistle. "Man, that's messed up. I'll never understand you women."

"Who sent it to you?"

"One of the guys in my dorm. I guess it's flying around campus 'cause someone found out she used to date Sean."

I groaned. This was bad.

Mike went on. "I can't believe Sean was so into her. He usually has really high standards."

"Mike! I told you, they Photoshopped it. They spliced her head onto some Internet chick's body."

"If you say so. It's just pretty nasty, you know? It really looks like it's her."

"Yeah, that's the problem."

The owner, Gino, a balding man with a stoop and a heavy Italian accent, came over to our table. He had this habit of clasping his hands as if he were begging or praying, which Mike and I usually found hilarious. But today nothing seemed funny to me.

"And what do you like for lunch?" Gino held up a finger. "You must not order the pancetta omelet. It is what everybody is ordering, and now we have no more."

"The prosciutto panino?" said Mike.

Gino nodded and glanced at me. I had lost my appetite. "A cappuccino, please."

Mike gave me a questioning look as Gino walked away. "Thought you were hungry."

I touched the picture. "I don't really feel like eating anymore."

"Yeah, it's pretty nasty," Mike agreed. "The scar and all."

"That's not what I meant."

"Her thighs? You're right, they're even worse. They look like they got run over by a bunch of linemen in cleats. She ought to be knocking down the doors of some plastic surgeon."

I stared at Mike, shocked. Had he really just said that?

I knew a lot of men thought of women in those terms, but not men I wanted to be with. The fact that Mike could miss what was really disgusting about the whole debacle made me feel sick.

I could only imagine what Ruby's day at school was like today.

I thanked Gino absentmindedly as he set down my drink. When he walked away, I lifted the cappuccino and drained it in two long gulps.

Mike stared. "You got any taste buds left?"

I nodded, digging in my purse, and tossed a ten on the table. "I'm not in the mood for this right now. I'm taking off."

"Why?"

"What you just said was disgusting."

"What? The thing about the cleats?"

"The whole thing. You're totally missing the point." I gestured helplessly. How could I explain that little statements like that can give you a glimpse into a person's soul?

"What point?"

"The point that it's not about the woman's body! So what if she has cellulite! So what?"

"Well, it's nasty! She's putting herself out there online; why shouldn't I comment about it?"

"Look, the stuff you were saying . . . that scar is from having a *baby*. And most women have cellulite, Mike."

He looked at me and said unconvincingly, "Oh, hey, sorry. There's nothing wrong with cellulite. You're right."

"The point is, this is sick because people are trying to hurt Ruby by putting this out there."

"You're right, you're right," he said. But I could tell he still didn't get it.

I could have screamed in frustration. "You know what? We should have broken up after the Tippecanoe thing. Let's not waste any more of each other's time."

Mike's eyes widened.

I gathered steam. "I really don't think we're right for each other."

"I heard you the first time," he said sharply.

"Sorry."

We were both quiet for a moment. Then Mike said, "Babe, don't do this."

I wavered, but somewhere deep down I knew I had to keep going. "Look, think about it. You're not really in love with me." And as I said it, I realized that it was true. I'd known it for a while now.

"I never said I was."

"Yes, you did."

"No, I didn't."

We stared at each other.

Suddenly I was hit with the ludicrousness of the situation. I stood and shouldered my bag. "I rest my case."

"Stella, don't."

I pretended not to hear him and walked out.

As I headed to my car, the air felt startlingly crisp and clean. I drew in a deep lungful and smiled.

Chapter Twenty-four

Monday at school Ruby was waiting by my locker after homeroom. Her hair was pulled back in a messy ponytail, and there were dark circles under her eyes. For once she was wearing sweats. She held one of those cardboard take-out trays loaded with three to-go cups and a couple of pastry bags.

She shoved it toward me. "The two on that side are yours. I didn't know if you'd want a latte or a mocha, so I got both. The coffee cake is low-fat."

I took the container labeled LATTE and cradled it against my chest. "Thanks."

"No problem."

We studied each other for a moment. Ruby said, "I'm sorry. I shouldn't have taken you along for that."

"It's okay," I said.

"Really?" She sounded hopeful.

"Really."

Looking relieved, she shook the pastries from their bags.

My eyes widened as she took an enormous bite of a white chocolate English toffee bar. "You feeling okay?"

Ruby shrugged. "You only live once. What are you complaining about? I got low-fat for you."

"Nothing, it's just good to see you eating." Other than the toffee bar, she had been smoking more lately and eating less. Her hips poked out of her low-riders at sharp angles, and her cheekbones looked more pronounced.

She gave me a crumb-filled smile.

The bell rang, and we headed for English. We passed Stacy and Emma in the hall, and they smirked at Ruby and started talking in low voices to each other.

"They've been busy online," Ruby commented.

I snuck a glance at her, surprised at how calm she sounded.

"My phone's ringing off the hook. I think it's mostly high school idiots, playing around. The woman in the picture is so nasty I doubt anyone would actually go for her."

"You didn't call the cops?"

Ruby snorted. "The cops wouldn't help. They can't prove anything."

"Maybe they could trace who posted it first," I suggested.

Ruby shook her head. "That would just blow it up even bigger."

"Did you tell Kenneth?"

"No, he doesn't care about high school drama."

I stared at her walking beside me. "I have to say, you're taking this whole thing really well."

"That's because I have a plan."

"What are you talking about?"

"I can't tell you, because then I would have to kill you." Ruby winked and pushed open the door to English class.

It's not an exaggeration to say that every single eye followed her as she took her seat. Even Kenny Mackinaw and Haley Mitchell, prize nerds, watched her walk in.

Ruby didn't miss it.

"Kenny, you got a thing for doughy chicks with C-sections?" she asked loud enough for everyone to hear. "Because I heard you've been looking at some dirty pictures."

Kenny blushed to the roots of his hair, and the whole class burst out laughing.

Mrs. Leland chose that moment to walk in. She glanced around. "Somebody want to let me in on the joke?"

Nobody said a word, but a few titters kept rolling. Looking innocent, Ruby took her seat and arranged her papers on the desk. I felt as proud as if she'd just made honor roll.

Mrs. Leland gave an uncertain smile. "All right, then. Let's take out our essays." Papers rustled and the focus shifted, but I was under no illusion that things would stay cool. Ruby wouldn't have mentioned a plan if she didn't intend to deliver.

I tore out a sheet of notebook paper and scribbled, "You have to tell me what you're going to do. I'm dying." I slid it to her desk.

Ruby scanned the paper, then shook her head and mouthed, "You'll see." She tore a strip off the note, rolled it into a tiny ball, and mimicked eating it.

By lunch I was highly anxious. I intercepted Ruby at her locker, my off-campus pass in hand. "You got me Starbucks earlier, so let me get lunch. We can go to World Wraps."

"Okay. I gotta do something in the quad really fast, but then we can go."

I grabbed her arm. "Ruby, if you just let it end here, they'll probably quit. Be the big one."

She shook me off. "Chill. You don't even know what I'm going to do. And no, they won't. Remember Utah? The broken wrists?"

I didn't have a comeback for that.

My stomach twisted like a pit of snakes as I fell into step next to her, but I had a strange peace, too. Whatever happened, I knew whose side I was on this time.

The halls were like a larger version of English class: heads swiveled and waves of chatter followed us. We passed Christine and Beth, and Christine gave me a disgusted look. Beth avoided my eyes, as usual.

Ruby barely seemed to notice.

A thought sent sudden chills up my spine. "You don't have a gun or something, do you?" I whispered.

She laughed out loud. "No, Mom. Relax, okay? You want to wait for me in the parking lot?"

I shook my head. This was something I had to do, as much for me as for her.

Ruby went directly to the popular tables. Amazing how such a noisy, crowded area could fall silent so quickly. Lisa sidled closer to her boyfriend, Tim, like maybe Ruby was going to punch her again. Every head turned in our direction. Someone must have spotted Ruby on the way, because a flood of kids poured onto the quad after us, following the tantalizing smell of blood before a fight.

I felt totally exposed.

Ruby stepped onto a bench at one of the lunch tables, and the few kids sitting there scattered like pigeons. Ruby stuck her hands on her hips and surveyed the crowd with a grin. "Hey, all you porn-lovers! You're into some sick stuff, you know that? C-sections and black leather?" She yanked her shirt up to the base of her breasts and pushed her sweats down to her bikini line, revealing her perfect stomach: defined and curvy, with a tiny silver belly ring and no sign of cellulite or scars. "I know it's going to disappoint you, but I want you to know: the picture you've been looking at isn't actually me. Rhetta Nakamura paid me a hundred bucks for a head shot so she could splice it on top of her body and see what she might look like if she didn't have an ass from the neck up."

Laughter rolled across the quad, and Ruby swayed her hips, playing to the audience. A wolf whistle cut the air.

From the hallway, the yard monitor broke into a trot, speaking into her walkie-talkie.

Ruby jumped down lightly and adjusted her shirt.

The monitor finally got through the crowd and placed a hand on Ruby's arm. "You need to come to the office."

"Get off me." Ruby shook her arm free, but there was no real anger in her voice. She winked at me. "Guess we'll have to do World Wraps tomorrow, Stel."

I beamed. "If you're not suspended."

As she gave me a mock-princess wave, a word popped into my mind: *unsinkable*. I watched as the monitor led her away.

"You little bitch." I turned to find Emma, arms crossed,

staring at me. Her friends were materializing around her: Rhetta, Stacy, and a layer of followers behind them. Brianna was there, too. That hurt.

Adrenaline tensed my limbs.

"Rhetta's been your friend since grade school, and you let that bitch talk crap about her?" Stacy didn't have the tough thing down as well as Rhetta and Emma, but she was trying.

"Ruby says what she wants, and I don't think Rhetta considers herself my friend," I said as calmly as I could.

Rhetta cocked her head to one side. "That kind of hurts my feelings. You know, you used to be okay, Stella. But people have been talking about you since you started hanging out with that whore. You guys dykes? Or are you just a little wanna-be? I mean, you were always a follower, but nobody figured you'd pick such a trashy slut for a mentor."

I felt a wave of nausea. It wasn't the words so much. Six months ago I would have listed all of them among my larger circle of friends.

"You really screwed up," Emma said softly. "You should have told us what she was going to do. And you let her punch Lisa that time. Here's some advice: don't show your face at graduation."

"Tell your bitch friend not to show up, either," added Stacy.

"Go to hell." I tried to walk away, but the circle tightened, blocking me. I felt their anger. My eyes traveled the hostile faces, and I made a split-second decision: I broke past Stacy with a fierce jab of my elbow.

"Get her!" someone hissed.

I heard Rhetta answer as I began to run. "Let her go. We'll wait until graduation. We don't need anything on our school records." My heart was racing as I weaved through confused freshmen and sophomores.

Ruby was right. They had never been my friends.

Chapter Twenty-five

"They are evil incarnate." Ruby rolled onto her back and plucked a cigarette from behind her ear. She flicked her lighter with a heavy sigh and sucked on the cigarette until the tip glowed red. Somehow, Gina hadn't noticed that Ruby didn't even pretend not to smoke in the house anymore. "So they plan to do something to us at graduation, huh? Now I'll actually have to go."

"You weren't going to walk?" I asked incredulously.

Ruby rolled her eyes. "Give me a break. Rent a black sack so I can boil to death for two hours and listen to DeVries butcher a speech? Probably not."

"But it's a big deal! It's like a wedding or something. People give you money and stuff."

"Who? Gina?"

Suddenly I realized that Ruby didn't have the web of aunts and uncles that I had, people who lived far away but wouldn't miss sending a gift for a birthday or Christmas, and certainly not graduation. "People," I said lamely.

"Well, nobody's giving *me* any money, I promise you that. I'm definitely not walking. But I'll go so you don't have to deal with those bitches alone. You think your family would care if I sat with them?"

"They'd *love* if you sat with them."

"Okay, then. I can't believe Nakamura thinks she's going to mess with us at graduation. What a cold bitch." Ruby stared at the ceiling, blowing smoke rings. "Hey, would you be mad if I did a couple lines right now?"

I glanced at Ruby. This was the second time since the heroin incident that she'd asked how I felt about her getting high. Something had definitely changed. "I won't be mad, but I'll probably go home."

Ruby pouted. "I'm tired."

"So drink coffee like a normal person."

"Coffee's not as fun." Ruby scraped herself off the bed and rooted around for her purse. "Fine, but you're paying, and I'm getting a triple."

"Sounds good to me."

We went outside to the car and I drove us to the Chocolate Company, feeling cheerful.

The Chocolate Company was packed. We had to circle the lot a couple times, but we finally found a spot.

Ruby rolled her eyes as we walked in. "Great. Bet it takes us at least thirty minutes to even get in our order." Then she frowned. I followed her eyes: Kenneth, sitting at a table in the corner, reading a magazine.

As if he could feel her gaze, he looked up; and there was

an odd, awkward moment of surprise. He set down his magazine and hurried to join us.

"Hi, baby!" He kissed Ruby's cheek.

Ruby looked at him strangely. "I thought you had to take your dad to the doctor."

"He's being stubborn. Refused to get out of bed. I finally got tired of fighting with him and rescheduled."

"That sucks," Ruby said.

"Yeah, he's like a little kid about going to the doctor. I should probably start bribing him with lollipops or something. What are you girls drinking? Sit down and let me order for you. The line is crawling."

Ruby considered. "A triple Americano."

"I'll have a mocha. Thanks." I dug in my purse for some money, but Kenneth waved me away. Ruby squeezed his hand, and we went to wait at the table, which was littered with an empty coffee cup and a stack of magazines: *Maxim, Men's Health*, and *Newsweek*.

"It's gotta be hard taking care of his dad," I commented.

"You don't even know. He's like a nanny and a maid wrapped into one. He cleans his house, cooks for him, reads to him, takes him on walks, and like a thousand other things."

"If he's so rich, why doesn't he just pay somebody to do that stuff?"

Ruby paused. "Huh. I don't know. Maybe he doesn't trust anybody else to do it right. He loves his dad a lot."

I tried to imagine Mom helpless and old. I wouldn't necessarily trust a stranger to take care of her, either; but I'd make Jackie and Marcus pull their weight for sure. "Does he have any brothers and sisters?"

Ruby shook her head. "He's an only child. It's a lot of pressure."

"What are you two whispering about?" Kenneth set down our drinks and pulled out his chair.

"How did you get through the line so fast?" Ruby demanded.

He winked. "I have my ways."

I glanced at the barista, a pretty blond girl. *Yeah, he's got his ways,* I thought.

"So what were you talking about?" he asked again. "You looked intense."

"Debating on what size halo to give you for taking care of your dad so well," Ruby told him.

Kenneth shrugged. "It's what anyone would do."

"How long has he had Alzheimer's?" I asked.

"He's been deteriorating for the last five years. It's the kind of disease that just keeps getting worse until finally you don't even know your own name. Getting lost is a huge problem. One time I took my eyes off him for five seconds in the mall, and he wandered out into the street. I had to call the police. We finally found him in someone's house half a mile down the road."

"Were they home?" asked Ruby.

"Well, not when he went in, but they got home while he was still there. They found him sitting at the kitchen table, eating leftovers from their fridge."

"It's strange that they would leave their door open," I said.

"Well, this *is* small town, U.S.A. Hey, no more about my dad. I'm on a water break from him." Kenneth winked and reached across the table to scoop up the tiny pendant that lay on Ruby's chest. "Where did you get this beautiful necklace?"

"Oh, this handsome man gave it to me."

I just about puked.

"You like it?" Ruby turned to show me. "It's aquamarine."

I pretended to admire the necklace. It was a twist of silver wire around a sparkling blue stone, sort of modern looking but still delicate. "It's beautiful," I admitted.

"He has good taste," said Ruby.

"Especially in women," Kenneth added with another wink.

I looked back and forth between the two of them. "You guys need to cut it out or I'm going to hurl."

"Sorry, we're still in the initial euphoric stage," said Kenneth.

"I don't think it's a stage," said Ruby.

"You haven't been in as many relationships as I have, babe. But hopefully we'll be able to sustain it for a nice long time before we start picking our noses around each other and wandering around the house in the same T-shirt every day."

I had to giggle. Kenneth's humor was a small redeeming point.

Kenneth glanced at his watch. "Water break is over. I have to get back to Dad. What are you girls doing today? You should go shopping. Ruby needs something to wear for this weekend."

"Kenneth is taking me to see Blue Man Group in Chicago," Ruby told me.

Kenneth pulled a wad of bills from his pocket and peeled off a few, pressing them into Ruby's hand. "Get something sophisticated but not boring." He touched her mid-thigh. "No shorter than this." Then he moved his hand down a couple of inches. "But no longer than this."

"What color?" asked Ruby.

"I'm wearing gray, so stick to black or blue or red. Definitely don't go brown."

"We like to complement each other," Ruby informed me.

I couldn't believe how much control she was giving him. "Hmmm" seemed the safest thing to say.

"Bye, baby." Ruby leaned over to kiss Kenneth. I stared out the window; but I couldn't help noticing the intimacy of it, as if they'd been together much longer than a few months.

Kenneth gave me a little wave, and we watched as he walked through the door and down the street with the casual confidence of a man who knows exactly how good-looking he is.

I couldn't help myself. "Does he always tell you how to dress?"

Ruby looked at me coolly. "How about 'That was so sweet of Kenneth to get us coffee,' or 'How nice that he wants us to go shopping,' or 'He's such a great guy for taking care of his dad'?"

"Sorry," I said defiantly, "but the thing about the skirt stuck out to me. I'm just asking."

"Well, for your information, I *like* it when he gives input on what I wear. It proves he's not just some hunk of testosterone that can't see past his own biceps."

"He did flex for us that one time at LaSalle."

"What?"

"Never mind."

Ruby leaned forward on her elbows and gave me a hard stare. "You're still hung up on the age thing, and you're never going to get past it, are you?"

"Maybe not," I admitted. "And the coke. You're getting all twitchy lately. How can I like a guy who gives you that stuff?"

"Hey, I wanted to do some earlier today and I didn't for you!"

I held up my hands. "Fair enough."

"I probably shouldn't do so much," Ruby said, her tone softer. "But that's my choice, not Kenneth's. I'd get it somewhere else if I didn't get it from him. You know that."

I nodded. Sad but true.

"And the age thing is what it is. I don't expect you to understand, but it's really not as weird as you think. If you could just step out of your—"

"Cultural bubble," I interrupted. "Yeah, I know. I've heard this lecture before."

"Well, it's true."

"Okay, but we're not living in dynastic China or the Middle East. We're in twenty-first century America."

"Well, maybe twenty-first century America needs to stop being so uptight."

"'Maybe twenty-first century America needs to stop being so uptight,'" I repeated in a high-pitched, whiny voice because I had no other reply.

We both burst out giggling.

"Just slow down on the coke, okay?" I added. "Seriously."

In answer, Ruby closed one nostril with a finger and gave a long, wicked sniff.

Chapter Twenty-six

During the last month and a half of school (in Indiana, we're on the farmers' schedule, so we get out in late May), I had dual obsessions fighting for space in my brain: graduation and the missing letter from Notre Dame.

Rhetta, Emma, and the others had been so smug that I knew they were cooking up some elaborate piece of evil. The only thing that kept me from panicking was the knowledge that whatever happened, Ruby would be there with me.

As for the letter, there had been a mix-up in admissions at Notre Dame, and decision letters were being mailed a few weeks late. It was both torture and a lifeboat: I still had something to hope for.

Then, on Wednesday afternoon two weeks before commencement I came home to find Mom waiting on the couch. She had a cup of tea in one hand and was lying back with her feet up, but I could tell the second I walked in that something was up.

Her eyes were bright with anticipation.

"Hi, sweetie." She patted the couch next to her. "Come sit."

I dropped my bag and walked over warily. "What?"

"What do you mean, what? I'm just asking you to sit down."

"Mom."

She couldn't contain her smile. "Okay, you can see right through me. Here, open it." She thrust an envelope at me.

My hands closed over it automatically, and I looked down, afraid to turn it over. It was too thin, too small.

"I didn't know you applied to Notre Dame! It would be so exciting to have you stay here in South Bend!" Mom's eyes were literally teary. "I've been worrying about how much I was going to miss you!"

"How would you know if I applied anywhere at all? It's not like you asked," I snapped, already dreading what the letter might say.

Mom looked stung. "Yes, I did. I asked in the fall, and you said not to bother you about it. You said you had it handled."

"Yeah, well, maybe I didn't." I dug my fingers into the envelope, wanting to rip it to shreds without even opening it.

"Honey, what's wrong? Can't you please open it? You did apply, didn't you?"

I turned over the envelope and slid my finger under the flap, pulling it open. There was a single sheet inside. Torture to even look.

Dear Ms. Chavez:

We regret to inform you that . . .

I crumpled the letter into a ball and held it in my fist. "I didn't get in."

"Oh, honey." Mom opened her arms, but for once I had no desire to walk into them. "Well, I'm sure you'll get into one of the other colleges you applied to."

"Why would I get in? Other kids got SAT prep classes and private consultants. Their parents took them to see campuses and meet admissions people."

Tears shone in Mom's eyes. "I'm sorry, honey. I didn't know." She gestured helplessly. "I never went to college myself. I don't know about these things."

"Besides, I didn't apply anywhere else," I went on cruelly. "How am I supposed to leave you guys? Who would do all the cleaning around here and take care of Marcus and Jackie? You work all the time."

Mom stared at me, horrified. "You didn't apply anywhere else? And because of *us*?"

I shook my head.

"Nobody asked you to do that! You know I said you could go wherever you wanted! I've been telling you that for years."

"What, am I supposed to leave Jackie and Marcus to raise themselves?"

Mom's cheeks reddened. "Do you think for one second that I am not perfectly capable of handling Jackie and Marcus on my own? I've been raising all three of you! Do you know how hard I've worked so you *could* go to college? I didn't think I needed to babysit you!"

"Well, maybe you were wrong."

I was so, so angry and knew I was being completely unfair.

It was my own stupid fault. I should have hugged my mom, told her I was sorry. But all I could bring myself to do was walk woodenly up the stairs to my room, the letter still clenched in my hand.

In my bed, I forced myself to uncrumple the letter and read it through. It was brief and to the point. I was not the right match for Notre Dame, but they hoped I would find a good university for me. They had to turn away many applicants each year. They encouraged me to reapply if I was still interested next year.

I tossed the paper to the floor and lay on my back, not moving.

I had gambled like an idiot and lost. What the hell was I going to do now?

A series of cliché images flew through my head: me on a plane to God knows where. Partying with hot foreign men. Backpacking through the jungle. Hitchhiking on a dirt road. Joining the Peace Corps.

The only thing I could not imagine was staying here, in South Bend, for one minute past graduation.

The pull to leave was so strong that I wondered if I would've been happy if I *had* gotten into Notre Dame. Suddenly it all made me feel so claustrophobic I wanted to choke: the town, Mike, my family, the strip malls and chain restaurants, even the few pretty points like Lake Michigan.

I had to get out of the house. I fumbled next to the bed for the cordless and called Ruby, praying she would answer.

"Can I come over?" I barked when she answered the phone.

"Whoa, you okay?"

"I'm fine. Can I come over?"

"Um, you are obviously not fine. But yes, come over."

I hung up without saying good-bye and rolled off the bed. I grabbed my purse and pocketed the car keys. Mom was sitting on the couch where I'd left her. I didn't meet her eyes as I walked by. "I'm going to Ruby's."

"Stella, we need to talk."

"I'm going to Ruby's."

I caught Mom's face crumpling before I slammed the door, sick to my stomach. I barely remember driving to Ruby's; I was on total autopilot.

The truth was sinking in, one layer at a time: I was not going to college next fall.

3.8 GPA, for nothing. Great SATs, for nothing. My whole life up in the air. What had I done?

I did an awful parallel park in front of Ruby's house, almost hitting the bumper of the truck in front of me, and tore up the steps. I wanted to jump out of my own skin.

When Ruby answered the door, she took one look at me and said, "Is your family okay?"

I nodded and pried off my shoes.

"Want a drink? You look like you need a drink." Ruby was already fishing in the liquor cabinet, setting a bottle of Bailey's and a bottle of Ketel One on the table. She poured generous amounts of each into two glasses, dropped in a few ice cubes, stirred them with her finger, and handed me one. "What happened?"

"I didn't get into Notre Dame."

She stared at me briefly, then wiped her hands on her pants. "So?"

"So I guess I'm not going to college next year," I said grimly.

"That's the only place you applied?"

"Yes."

"Oh," she said, frowning. "Well, then you're right; you're not going to college next year."

"That's all you can say?"

"What do you want me to say? You messed up. Now you're paying for it. We all do that sometimes. But it's really not that big a deal. Just do something so kick-ass this coming year that you can write your essays about it and get in wherever you want to. That's *my* strategy."

I took a swig of my drink. "I don't have a sugar daddy taking me to Asia."

"Maybe we can find you one. Go to Vegas or something."

"No thanks."

"Isn't there something you've always wanted to do? Something crazy and fun?"

"You're thinking like yourself. Think like me for a change."

"Okay, then I'll just sit in South Bend for the rest of my life, weighed down by imaginary responsibilities."

I winced.

Ruby looked worried. "Don't listen to me; I'm stupid. Come on, let's get your mind off it. Drink that fast, and we'll go get snakebites at Fiddler's Hearth. It'll help to be out."

"Yeah, around a bunch of Notre Dame students," I said, rolling my eyes. But really, it wasn't a bad idea. I needed noise, distraction. I tossed back the rest of the drink. "Can I borrow a scarf?"

"Of course. Just let me change and we'll go." I followed Ruby to her bedroom and sank into her beanbag chair. The alcohol had made a tiny dent in my stress. Ruby dabbed on makeup, sifting through tangled clothes on the floor.

"We're just going out to eat. You don't have to look like a supermodel," I said.

"What if we run into Kenneth?"

I rolled my eyes. "Is he all you think about?"

"I can't help it. I'm in love." Ruby laid a black sweater and jeans on her bed and shrugged her sweatshirt over her head.

I gasped. Her chest was crisscrossed with thin, red cuts. They were evenly spaced and symmetrical: three running vertically and a single horizontal line slicing through the middle. "Did you have *surgery?*" I asked, shocked.

Ruby's arms jerked to cover her chest, and she turned around, hurrying to tug the black sweater over her head. Her silence sent chills up my spine.

"Ruby, what happened?"

She turned, feigning nonchalance as she picked up a compact. "Nothing."

"Are you a *cutter?*"

"Ew! No!"

"Then tell me what they are."

She cast me an irritated look. "Ever heard the term M.Y.O.B.?"

"That doesn't apply when my best friend is covered in cuts."

Ruby stopped fiddling. "Am I really your best friend?"

"Do you even have to ask?"

"Well, shucks, that's sweet," she said in a hillbilly accent.

"Don't try to distract me. What happened?"

"You'll be judgmental."

"No, I won't," I lied.

"Okay, but no lectures."

"I promise."

"Have you ever heard of blood sport?"

My skin crawled. "No."

"It's this sex thing. It doesn't hurt or anything, and it doesn't leave scars. You just give each other really *light* cuts, like paper cuts."

"What?"

Ruby blushed. "You said no lectures."

"I'm not lecturing. I just . . . this is supposed to be sexy?"

"Yes. Now can we talk about something else?"

But I wasn't done. I had barely started processing. "You mean you let Kenneth *cut* you because he gets off on it?"

"I like it, too."

"Why?"

Ruby huffed in exasperation. "Why not? Sex is like food. You can't explain somebody's taste."

I gaped at her. I was feeling nauseous and panicky. This was bad. But I had to cover up how freaked out I was or she wouldn't tell me anything else. I tried to keep my voice light. "Okay, but it's easy to understand why everybody likes ice cream and pizza, whereas stuff like raw liver is harder to explain. What's good about raw liver? That's what I'm asking."

"If you don't know already, you'll never understand."

"Try."

"I like being out of control for once."

I must have looked confused, because she gestured impatiently. "You think I'm out of control, but I'm not. I'm wild. There's a difference. Look, I'm always in control, believe me. I barely know how I'm feeling half the time, I'm so in control."

I nodded, understanding too well.

Ruby went on. "I like *feeling* things. So do most people. But for me it takes more. Like think of hot sauce. It's all relative. Mild salsa is a ten on some people's spice scale, while Thai people think raw jalapeños are about a five. I'm like a Thai person."

"You need intensity in order to really feel things."

Ruby nodded. "Why do you think I like coke? It's intense. Don't you get it?"

Suddenly, I *did* get it. It might be nice to go over the edge about something. I wasn't sure I ever really had.

Ruby pulled on her jacket. "Can we please go now? I'm dying of hunger, and you're making me psychoanalyze myself. That's not very nice."

"Yeah, okay."

The walk was long and cold, and I couldn't get the image of those awful cuts out of my head. With each passing minute, Ruby's explanation was making less and less sense. How could someone get off on hurting someone else? Or on being hurt? It was twisted.

Finally we got to Fiddler's Hearth, which was hot, noisy, and crammed with Notre Dame grad students—mostly art and English types, from the looks of their scruffy clothes and lanky hair. I ordered fish and chips, and Ruby ordered us snakebites—a lethal mixture of cider and lager—but I couldn't enjoy mine.

"I knew you would judge me," Ruby said, watching me over the rim of her glass.

"What?"

"You've barely said one word since we left the house. You're all caught up in your own head, *judging.*"

"Sorry I'm worried that my best friend's boyfriend belongs in *Silence of the Lambs*," I snapped.

There was a moment when it could have gone either way. But then Ruby started to giggle. Pretty soon we were both laughing hysterically. *"Clariiiiice* . . . ," intoned Ruby, and that set us off even harder. Then the fish and chips arrived, and I made an effort to seem more chatty and upbeat.

But on the inside I was still sick.

Chapter Twenty-seven

The next morning reality hit me like a fist. I woke up late nestled in a pile of blankets on Ruby's floor to a slicing headache and dull, stinging vision. My eyes *felt* red. The sun slipping under the blinds was too bright for morning; it had to be past noon.

I glanced over and saw that Ruby was still asleep, her arm hanging off the bed and fingers grazing the floor. Her blanket was pulled up over her breasts, but I could make out the tips of the cuts on her chest. My stomach turned as everything flooded back. I hadn't gotten into Notre Dame, and this pervert was hurting my friend.

What if he decided to do something even worse?

I climbed out of the blankets, treading lightly, though Ruby could sleep through an air raid. My clothes stank of smoke, so I pulled on a pair of Ruby's sweats and a hoodie. I felt shaken and ill. I had to do something, but I didn't know what. At the moment, the main thing was to get out of there.

Downstairs, Gina was sipping coffee on the couch, a newspaper spread out in front of her. She glanced up. "Morning."

"Good morning." For a second I considered telling her about the cuts, but then I decided not to. It was Thursday; if she didn't even care that we weren't in school, what kind of help would she be with Kenneth? Also, Ruby would be eighteen in a week, at which point whatever power Gina had would evaporate.

"Fresh coffee?" Gina pointed toward the kitchen. Her hair was pulled up in a loose bun, and she was wearing a dark blue kimono embroidered with blossoms. Her slim ankles were crossed on the coffee table, revealing perfectly painted toes. She already had on full makeup.

How much effort did it take to be her?

An image of my mom, hair wild and curly, popped into my mind. She'd be in her threadbare flannel robe right now, wandering around the kitchen with a cup of tea.

I shook my head. "No thanks. I have to go. Would you tell Ruby I said bye?"

"Sure thing, honey. Have a nice day." Gina wiggled her fingers at me as I passed the couch.

Outside it was glorious, finally real spring. Melted snow trickled through the gutters, and the sky was a bright, endless wash of blue. I got in my car and started toward Lula's.

School was not an option for the day.

As I waited in line for my coffee, I tried to figure out what to do. If Ruby wasn't so close to eighteen, I could tell my mom, or a teacher, or somebody who could press charges against Kenneth for statutory rape. But by the time the case got to court, Ruby would be a consenting adult. Besides, I didn't want the police involved, because Ruby could get in trouble, too—if they found out about the drugs.

That left convincing Ruby to leave Kenneth—*not* going to happen—or convincing Kenneth to leave Ruby.

A wisp of an idea began to form in my mind.

Kenneth was obviously a selfish egomaniac. If I could convince him that it was in his own best interest to stay away from Ruby, he might go along with it. And here I had some leverage: maybe the threat of cops would be enough to scare him off. Also, Kenneth's dad didn't know how old Ruby was, or what a pervert and cokehead Kenneth was. Both pieces of information, I suspected, were not things Kenneth would want advertised to his family.

And if the threat of telling the cops or his dad wasn't enough, I would go through with it. I would call the police to save my friend.

But even at seventy or whatever he was, Kenneth's dad might have some influence if I could catch him when he was clear minded. Hadn't Ruby said they lived next door to each other? Then he wouldn't be hard to find, because I knew where Kenneth lived. I'd given Ruby a ride to his house. Finding his dad would be a matter of knocking on the two doors on either side of Kenneth's house.

I latched onto the idea like a lifeboat.

"A quadruple latte?" the barista asked with raised eyebrows when I ordered. "You're gonna get the shakes."

"That's okay. I need them right now." I slid a dollar into the tip jar and gathered a handful of sugar packets.

I really did need four espressos. I hadn't felt so gross since the eighth-grade dance, when Christine and Elsa convinced me to drink half a bottle of Captain Morgan.

I found a seat by the window and collapsed into a comfy couch. After draining about half my latte, my brain kicked into higher gear. I needed to talk to Kenneth face-to-face. On the phone it would be too easy for him to hang up on me; plus, I didn't have his number.

I had to stop by his house. It was the only way.

My fingers drummed the table. The barista was right: I was starting to feel shaky. I thought feebly that I must be insane or still drunk. Was I really going to try and blackmail Kenneth? When Ruby found out, she would kill me.

I conjured up an image of the cuts. It didn't matter what Ruby thought. What mattered was separating her from this sadistic freak before he really hurt her.

She'll just find another, my mind whispered, and I shivered.

It might be true, but I still had to do something. Kenneth was real; the cuts were real. *That* was what I had to deal with.

I ditched my drink and went to the car. It seemed important that I act now, before I lost courage. The wheel felt slick as I drove, and I realized with disgust that it was my own sweat.

What if Kenneth wasn't there? What if he was? What if he tried to hurt me? I punched in an Enya CD to relax, but the syrupy music was so at odds with my mood.

I switched to a heavy metal station. After a minute I realized the song was about a serial killer. Even under normal circumstances that would gross me out. I turned off the radio and just drove fast.

The houses in Kenneth's neighborhood were fat-cat: the

lawns looked as if nobody ever walked on them, and the houses were the perfect "homes" that so few people actually get to live in. I panicked a little, unsure if I'd made it to the right street; but then I spotted the hedge around Kenneth's two-story and felt relief plus a whole new kind of panic.

His car was in the driveway.

I parked along the curb across from his house and sat there, nerves jangling.

I wanted him to be home, didn't I?

I tried to calm myself by focusing on small details: the shiny blue tricycle sitting in the yard next to Kenneth's, the stone walkway to the front door, the ivy crawling gracefully up the wall like it had been arranged there by an artist. I tried to rehearse what I would say. Best to keep it simple and straightforward. Had to keep my composure. Had to let him see that I was serious.

My skin ached. Was I getting the flu?

I pressed my palms to the cool dashboard and prayed. *God, please let this go according to Your will. Please give me peace and put words in my mouth. Please protect Ruby. Mary, Mother of God, help me.* Finally I crossed myself and got out of the car.

I concentrated on deep breaths as I walked up the steps, then lifted the knocker and knocked twice. It occurred to me as the door swung open that I didn't have mace, a knife, or anything remotely useful for self-defense.

"Stella!" Kenneth's hair was messy, and he had sheet prints on his face. It might have been funny if I wasn't so close to hyperventilating. He was wearing a pair of blue flannel pajamas; and somehow, despite the sheet marks, he looked like an ID ad.

"Sorry, Ruby's not here. Were you looking for her?"

"No, I wanted to talk to you." I could barely hear my own voice.

Kenneth looked confused, but he stepped aside to let me in. "Sit down. You okay?"

"Um, yeah, thanks." The front door opened into the living room, and I sat stiffly in a black stuffed chair.

Ruby was right: the whole place was very "world imports," with masks on the wall and an honest to goodness zebra hide on the floor. The only hint of bachelordom was a massive flat screen with a video game console.

Kenneth sat on a long, low couch across from me. "What's going on? Is Ruby okay?"

"Yeah, Ruby is fine." I tried to find the words I'd practiced, but they disappeared. My mind was an aching blank. "I saw her cuts," I blurted out.

Kenneth's face tightened. The mask was sliding on, neutralizing his expression. "All right," he said.

"And I want you to stop seeing her. Or I'll call the cops, and I'll tell your dad what you're doing."

Kenneth blinked, the slow, flat blink of someone caught seriously off guard. "Stella, what Ruby and I do together is really none of your business."

"Yes, it is. You're hurting her. She's underage."

"In a week she won't be."

"She's still only eighteen."

"And I'm thirty. Twelve years is not a big difference in the grand scheme of things."

"I thought you were thirty-four."

"No. I'm thirty." But there was a funny look on Kenneth's

face when he said it that sent my sensors ringing.

"Twelve years is a big difference when one of you isn't even twenty-one."

Kenneth ran a hand through his hair. "What the hell are— This is—never mind. Let me put it another way. I will *not* stop seeing Ruby. I'm in love with her. Whatever you do, I'm sure it'll seriously annoy both of us, but you won't accomplish any more than that." He leaned forward. "I get it that you're trying to protect your friend. And, believe it or not, I respect that. But you have to know that I would never hurt Ruby. You might not understand some of the . . . ways we express our affection, and that's fine; most people don't. But I wouldn't hurt her."

"You don't think it's hurting her to give her all that coke?"

I could tell from his reaction that I'd scored a point. His eyes widened, then he nodded slowly.

"All right. Maybe we need to cut back. But that's really none of your business."

"The police would think it's their business."

Kenneth gave me a cold stare. "Thanks for the warning. I'll make sure I'm ready for a visit. And don't threaten me. You could never pin anything tangible on either one of us. Besides, what do you think you'd accomplish? A police record for your friend just when she becomes a legal adult? Nice."

I felt my confidence slipping away. "I'm telling your dad, then." Even to my ears, it sounded stupid and babyish.

Kenneth sneered. "You don't know anything about my father."

"I know he lives next door!"

"No, he doesn't. I'm tired of this. Get out of my house." Kenneth stood and was at the door in a few quick steps. He threw it open, and I saw that he was dangerously close to losing his temper.

I got up and walked past him with as much dignity as I could muster. Then I nearly flew to my car. I turned the key in the ignition and peeled out, heart hammering. I was a failure. All I'd done was warn him.

And now Ruby would absolutely hate me.

Chapter Twenty-eight

When I pulled into my driveway, Mom's car was already there. She must have had a short shift. I checked my face in the rearview mirror: a little flushed and glassy-eyed, but basically normal. Mom wouldn't be happy to hear I skipped school, but I didn't have the energy to lie. I walked in to find her sitting on the living-room floor, sorting laundry.

She looked up in surprise. "You're home early. Is it a half day?"

I shook my head and burst into tears.

"Honey?" Mom stood, and in two quick steps she gathered me in her arms. She was still in her uniform, and I could smell the restaurant on her: fried food and baked goods and coffee.

She rocked back and forth, patting my back. "It's good to cry," she whispered in my ear. "Just get it out."

I sniffed, trying to get control of myself. I hate breaking down.

"Do you want some tea and popcorn? I'll get us some tea and popcorn."

"Mom, popcorn is not a panacea. I'll be fine."

"Well, sit with me for a minute. Come on."

"On the floor?"

"On the couch, if you insist, Your Majesty."

I sat.

Mom plopped next to me and pulled me against her shoulder. "I know this college thing is hard. And I want you to know that I've been thinking about everything you said, and— "

"It's not about college."

Mom looked alarmed. "Something else happened?"

"Nice weather we're having," I stalled.

"Stella."

I sighed. "Okay. Hypothetically, what if someone you love is in trouble, and you can't help them because they don't want to be helped?"

Mom gave a grim laugh. "I've been there a time or two."

"When?"

She looked at me as if I were stupid or crazy. "Your dad?"

"Oh, yeah."

"Here's what I can tell you: you can't save someone from themselves. That's up to them and God. I learned that the hard way."

"Dad and drugs?"

"Yes. Do you know how many times I checked him into rehab? But his heart never changed. Without a change of heart, it's useless. I should have left him, but I was too weak. I hung on until he left me."

"I don't think you're weak."

Mom gave me a curious look. "Believe me, I am. And it's only when you realize how weak you are that you can even start to be strong."

"Now you're preaching."

"I can't help it if the Bible is right."

I grinned. "Doesn't it also say we're supposed to help people?"

"Yes, but you have to remember God's big gift to us is free will. You have to allow people free will. This is about Ruby, right?"

"I said it's hypothetical."

"Okay, well, let me tell you something about Ruby, anyway. She's headstrong, and she's hurting very badly. But you can't walk her path for her."

I was surprised. "How do you know that about her?"

"Any halfway intelligent adult could tell that by spending two seconds with her, Stella. She has 'own agenda' written all over her face. But she's a good girl. I really do care about her."

"If she's so into doing whatever she wants, how come you don't mind that I hang out with her?"

"Because I trust you," Mom said simply. We were both quiet for a moment. "Listen, honey, did you ever think you might be drawn to Ruby because you want to help people like your dad? He was wild and hurting, too, and we couldn't save him. But you tried. You would beg him to 'be good.' And it made a bigger difference than anything I could do. He managed to clean up for almost six months one time when you asked him to."

I felt a dangerous layer of myself being peeled back, and I was suddenly angry. At Mom. "I don't want to talk about this."

"I'm sorry. I didn't mean to bring up bad memories."

"Then don't." But it was too late.

Memories of Papi, who I'd worked so hard to forget, were flooding in. Tall, rangy, lean. Strong brown hands. A homely, sweet face with the kindest eyes. His cheeks were scarred from acne during his teenage years. His beautiful thick black hair was always oiled and perfectly combed. He was funny, smart, a firecracker. He would tell jokes that Mom didn't get. Sometimes when the mood struck, he'd make tortillas from scratch, eyeballing the amounts of flour and lard and salt, patting and spinning the dough until perfect disks emerged. Once they were cooked, he'd load them up with black beans and cheese and eat six or seven at a sitting.

Papi could fix anything. His fingers knew the magical workings of nuts, bolts, cogs, and screws; and he handled them lovingly. I pictured his hands stained with grease, repairing discarded appliances. We used to have a working gramophone. A Hoover from the nineteen fifties. Once he dismantled a blender and spread out the pieces on a clean towel like a puzzle, and tried to teach Jackie and me to identify the parts that belonged together.

Papi did air-conditioning for a living. Later when he wasn't well enough to work every day, he would sometimes go to Lowe's or Home Depot and stand outside, waiting for contract work. White men picked him up and gave him cash to put in a fence, paint a room, or dig up weeds. He was never lazy, just sick—although a lot of people won't admit that addiction is a sickness.

It happened slowly but certainly, like the tide coming in.

The tendons in his neck got ropy and pronounced. I could see a vein flickering above his left eye. His cheeks were hollow. He got more absentminded.

Papi was there but not. There was no anger, no yelling, no hitting—none of the scary things you hear about. Just Papi getting farther and farther away, receding into himself until all we had left was a smiling, sad-eyed shell.

Then he left.

Was that why I felt so close to Ruby, so comfortable around her, so protective? I shuddered.

"Just don't fall in love with an addict or follow anyone bent on destroying themselves. It hurts too much," Mom said.

But I wondered if I already had, in a way. This fierce, tender protectiveness I felt for Ruby, as if she were my sister or my own child; what was it if not love?

"And remember," Mom went on, "God can turn anything that happens into good. You just have to give it to Him."

"That is so cryptic." I got up. "No offense, but I can't handle this conversation anymore."

"I'm sorry, honey," Mom said softly. "I know it's hard to hear."

I nodded. "I'm going to lie down for a while. I'm tired."

Upstairs I collapsed on my bed. Body, mind, soul—everything needed to check out for a while. I stuck a pillow under my knees and took a long swig from my water bottle. I could sleep for days. But just as I was beginning to drift, a thought snagged my consciousness. Kenneth said he was thirty. But Ruby thought he was thirty-four. He said his dad didn't live next door, but Ruby told me he'd bought the house specifically to live next to his dad.

Something wasn't fitting.

That blue tricycle in the yard next to Kenneth's didn't belong to an old man. What about the house on the other side? As hard as I tried, I couldn't conjure up an image. It was brick, that's all I could remember. Strangely, the thought brought me peace, and I was finally able to fall asleep.

Chapter Twenty-nine

I was awakened by a barely there sound, the whisper of fabric on fabric. But it jolted me to consciousness like an alarm. I sat upright. "Jackie!"

She whipped around, eyes enormous, my best blue shirt dangling out of her fist. "I was just putting this back."

"Like hell you were. Put it down now."

She regained composure and, with a smirk, opened her hand and let the shirt drop to the floor.

"Hang it up."

"You said, 'Put it down now'!" But she bent and picked it up, only to toss it on the dresser. It was better than the floor, I guess.

I squinted and ran a hand through what felt like a bush on my head. Jackie's eyes were rimmed in raccoon-black and her lipstick was a deep, vampire plum. "You look like a total gangbanger," I said in disgust. "Just put on some Lee Press-Ons and you'll be ready for the initiation."

Jackie stuck out a tongue streaked blue by some awful candy. "I hear they make you kill a sibling to get in."

I fell back in bed. "Oooh, I'm scared."

"Ruby called you three times."

"She did?"

"Yeah, she sounded funny. She said you should call her back the second you woke up."

My stomach tightened. "What time is it?"

"Seven. Mom left for work an hour ago."

"*Seven?*" I hoisted myself out of bed. I'd been crashed out all afternoon. Of course Ruby knew about my visit to Kenneth by now. She was probably trying to decide the best way to kill me.

"What's wrong? Is something going on with you and Ruby?" Jackie was watching me closely.

I scowled. I hated how psychic she was. "No. Not that it would be any of your business. Scram."

"Can I borrow your blue shirt?"

"The one you were trying to steal a second ago?"

Jackie nodded.

"No! Get out of here!"

With a sigh, she turned and left.

I unwrapped an ancient breath mint and sucked on it, trying to clear the asleep-too-long taste from my mouth. I couldn't avoid Ruby forever. But I made a split second decision: I would exhaust all options before I faced her.

I shoved my feet into my tennis shoes and hollered toward

Jackie's room, "If my shirt is gone when I get back, I'm cutting the butt out of your favorite jeans!"

"Where are you going?"

"None of your business!" I went downstairs, yanked the car key from the hook, and headed out the door.

A light rain was misting down, and I hurried to my car, chin tucked against my chest. It was already dark, and the streets were patchy with ice. Spring rains were dangerous when the temperatures dipped because those ice patches could send a vehicle fishtailing in a heartbeat.

I drove slowly back the same way I'd driven earlier. It felt like déjà vu as my headlights illuminated the route to Kenneth's house.

Kenneth's neighborhood looked different by night, though: the houses more impressive, the trees sweeping dark shadows on the ground. Several upstairs lights were on in Kenneth's house, and the house with the tricycle out front was glowing. The house on the east side—the one his dad might live in— was dark except for one small light in a downstairs window. As I watched, it flickered and dimmed, and I realized it was a television.

I parked a few car lengths from the house and rummaged under the seat, pulling out my ski cap. The rain was coming down harder now.

It was oddly exhilarating to creep along the side of the road, sticking to the shadows. I edged into the yard, hunching in a low, awkward gait to stay out of sight of the window. Please God, no dogs.

The house was a brick two-story with a hedge of hydrangeas

out front. There was a foot or so gap between the hydrangeas and the house, and I wedged myself between the bushes until I was up against the brick, sidling toward the window. I could hear curses and muted explosions as the light inside flickered dramatically.

When I got to the window, I inched forward, crouching, until just my forehead and eyes peeped over the sill. Inside was an older couple curled up together on an enormous couch facing a screen. I had a decent view of the woman: plump, somewhere in her fifties or sixties, with soft features and a blond bob. All I could make out of the man was the top of a balding head and a long, sweatshirt-clad arm wrapped around the woman's shoulder. The two of them were tucked under a blanket that seemed to be a giant knit picture of the American flag.

The room was dim, but I could see that it was very neat and comfortable in an Amish Acres–meets–Macy's sort of way: patchwork throws on overstuffed furniture, a wooden rocking chair, a grandfather clock, and a mantel full of high-end rag dolls. With the Amish settlement so close, lots of South Benders got into the Amish aesthetic; but they almost always added a little comfort and electricity.

The man stretched, and I saw a beaky profile. He looked Arabic—and nothing like Kenneth.

I scuttled back out of the bushes into the yard. Feeling fatalistic, I walked up the steps and rang the bell. As I waited, I glanced at Kenneth's house. No sign of life downstairs, just the same two windows lit on the second story. There was the sound of footsteps and the click of a bolt. I snatched off my ski cap as the door opened.

The man peered out at me. "Yes?"

I realized then that I had no idea what Kenneth's last name was. It was one of those awful times when your mouth hangs open but the words won't come. It didn't help that the man looked like some kind of retired athlete: fierce and ropy and at least six foot four. He was wearing a gray sweat suit and giant leather slippers. "Yes?" he repeated.

"Are you Kenneth's dad?" I blurted out.

The man frowned. "What? No. Who's Kenneth?"

"The guy who lives next door?"

The man glanced at Kenneth's house. "Oh, Ken Fairmont. No. Why on earth would you think that?"

"Because Kenneth said his dad lived next door. Do you know if he lives on the other side?"

There was a strange, loaded silence. Then the man said, "Bill Fairmont died years ago. Are you a relative?"

"Who is it, Tarik?" The woman from the couch padded into view. "We're not buying anything, dear."

"She's not selling anything. She wanted to know if I was Bill Fairmont."

"But Bill . . ." The woman glanced at the man.

"I already told her."

"I'm a little confused," she said. "Do you have the wrong house, sweetheart? Ken lives next door." The woman looked kind and grandma-dollish, with a bit too much rouge and a sweet, wrinkled mouth. In the porch light, her hair looked platinum.

"Actually . . ." I hovered for a second and then decided to go ahead and jump. "Okay. This is going to sound crazy, and I'm sorry to bother you guys at night like this. But I was wondering if I could ask you a few questions."

"Why don't you come inside and talk to us in here, dear? The cold air is coming in," the woman said.

The man shot her an irritated glance, which she ignored, pulling the door farther open.

I took a deep breath and stepped inside. In the entry hung a framed cross-stitch of the American flag. The wooden coatrack on the wall was so overloaded it looked seriously in danger of crashing to the ground.

"This way." The woman led me down a flagstone hall and into a bright, butter-yellow kitchen. Rag dolls were clustered on the counter around a miniature tea set, and a collection of porcelain pigs dressed in all kinds of painted costumes lined a display shelf above the stove.

I heard a bolt click behind us and then the man's heavy footsteps as he followed us into the kitchen. The woman pulled out a chair for me and took a seat herself at a round wooden table. "Now, let's start properly this time. I'm Mrs. Sharif and this is Mr. Sharif. And you are?"

Mr. Sharif pulled out a chair with a loud scrape and sat across from me.

I ran a tongue over dry lips. "I'm Stella Chavez. I'm a senior at Mishawaka High. I'm really sorry to bother you guys like this; but something weird is going on, and I'm trying to find out more about it. My friend . . . well, your neighbor Kenneth is dating my friend, and I think he's been lying to her."

Mr. and Mrs. Sharif exchanged glances. "How old is your friend, honey?" asked Mrs. Sharif.

"Almost eighteen."

Mrs. Sharif hit the table with the flat of her hand. "I *told* you, Tarik! But you said 'mind your own business.' Does she have reddish-blond hair, honey? Long?"

I nodded.

"There was that little black-haired gal before her that had to be high school aged, too. She had a *backpack* that one time, for goodness sake."

Mr. Sharif studied me, arms folded across his chest. "What do you think he's been lying about?"

"I'm not sure. A couple of things. Like, he said he lives here because he's taking care of his dad who lives next door and has Alzheimer's. And he told my friend he was thirty-four but then he told me he was thirty."

Mrs. Sharif flushed and said to her husband, "That disgusting man! What can we do? Can you get Robert involved?" She turned to me. "Tarik has a friend in the police department."

"Let the girl finish," Mr. Sharif said.

"I don't really know much else." My mind was scrambling over the two big things I did know but hadn't mentioned: the coke and the sex stuff. But this guy knew someone in the police department. I didn't want to get Ruby in trouble.

Mrs. Sharif leaned forward. "Let me tell you, honey, that man is a liar. He is at *least* forty, probably closer to forty-five; and his father has been dead for ten years. When did they move here, Tarik?"

"Almost twenty years ago. Ken was at IUSB, and they came here to be close to him. Then he dropped out."

"They spoiled him something awful," Mrs. Sharif said excitedly. "They owned a chain of Shell stations, and that boy never had to work a day in his life. First Helen passed and then Bill, and they left him everything. He's still never had a job, as far as we know."

"He told my friend he's a graphic designer for Microsoft," I said.

Mr. Sharif blew out a puff of air in disgust. "Graphic designer, my ass."

"Language, Tarik," warned Mrs. Sharif.

"Sorry. He's no graphic designer. He's been drawing on his father's trust fund for more than a decade. They left him the house free and clear."

"We've been wondering about his girlfriends for a while now." Mrs. Sharif shot her husband a glance. "Well, *I've* been wondering. Tarik told me it couldn't be as bad as I thought. But I know what a full-grown woman looks like, and that's not what that man has been dating."

"You said your friend is almost eighteen?" asked Mr. Sharif.

"In about a week."

"Would she be willing to testify in court that she had sexual relations with Ken before her eighteenth birthday?"

I shook my head. "No way. She thinks she's in love with him."

Mrs. Sharif made a distressed sound and covered her face. "Oh, that poor little idiot."

"Not much you can do then," said Mr. Sharif. "But I tell you what: she's not the first, and she won't be the last. I'll talk to my friend with South Bend PD, see if he can't put the fear of God in Ken, keep him away from other minors."

"That would be wonderful," I said fervently. "Thank you so much."

Mr. Sharif stood. "Don't get your hopes up. Once your friend is eighteen, she's legal. Best thing would be to tell her he's been lying to her. But lying seems to appeal to some women. If that's the case, she's a lost cause."

"I hope not." I stood, too. "Thanks again. You guys have helped me a lot."

Mrs. Sharif shook her head. "You young girls are so vulnerable. This culture, it eats you up and spits you out. Just little sex toys for men's imaginations."

"Violet . . ." Mr. Sharif sounded embarrassed.

"Well, it's true! Thank God we only have boys, both happily married. No offense, honey." Mrs. Sharif patted my back, and all three of us walked down the hall to the door. Mr. Sharif unlocked the door, and the security system beeped as I stepped outside.

"We'll pray for your poor friend," said Mrs. Sharif.

"Bye now," said Mr. Sharif.

I waved, then headed down the walkway toward the street.

Chapter Thirty

The digital clock on the dashboard read 8:40. No time like the present.

Still, I drove past Ruby's street and had to force myself to turn around several blocks later. She'd called three times, Jackie had said, and that was *before* I'd left the house to go to the Sharifs'. I wondered grimly if she would hit me with fire or ice.

But I had to try. She needed to know what I'd found out.

A large part of me was hoping Ruby *wouldn't* be home, but she answered right away when I knocked. "I thought it would be you," she said, stepping onto the porch.

So she wasn't even going to invite me in.

She hugged her chest and stared at me with a flat-lidded gaze. Ice, then.

"We need to talk." I hated how weak my voice sounded.

"You know, I thought so, too, most of the afternoon. But then I thought about what you did, and I decided we really don't have a lot to talk about. Actually, I'd appreciate it if you'd just leave."

I blinked, my traitorous eyes already stinging. "But I found out some stuff about Kenneth that you need to know."

"I don't really care what you found out about Kenneth. Now get off my porch." Ruby reached for the door.

"He's at least forty and his dad died ten years ago and he doesn't work for Microsoft at all!" I blurted out.

Ruby wheeled around, eyes wide. She knew I didn't lie.

"I talked to the neighbors. He dropped out of IUSB and then moved in with his parents. They died and left him everything. He's never had a real job. The neighbors said they've seen him with other high school girls."

Ruby's face began to crumple, but she made an effort and got control. "How do you know they're telling the truth?"

"They are! You can talk to them, too, and see for yourself. Their name is Sharif, and they live in the brick house next door. Look, I went because I'm worried about you. I knew something wasn't right about this guy. Ruby, he likes to *cut* you!"

"Fuck you!" Ruby screamed. "That's none of your business. You're just jealous! You're trying to screw up the one relationship I actually care about." She ripped open the door and ran inside, slamming it behind her so hard the frame shook.

I stared after her and burst into tears.

Why had I done any of it? For a second Ruby's words got inside my head: was I jealous in some subconscious way? Was I trying to sabotage what made her happy?

I ran down the steps and got in my car and peeled out hard.

I couldn't stop crying, but it started to feel more like rage than sadness. To hell with Ruby for not appreciating what I'd done for her. I *wasn't* jealous; I was the only friend she had, trying to protect her from a lying, abusive freak. I hit the wheel so hard my hand felt broken, but the pain cleared my head. I began to drive a little more sanely.

My crying slowed by the time I got home. I felt weary and washed out, but not crazy anymore. I plodded up the driveway and into the house, grateful that Mom was at work and Jackie out with friends, even though she was probably smoking dirt weed and vandalizing property.

The quiet house was like balm on my nerves. I flicked on the television and collapsed on the couch. That's when I noticed a folded note on the table. STEL, it read in capital letters. I unfolded it and a wrinkled ten fell out.

Dear Stel,

I know you're going to kill me, but I seriously couldn't find ANYTHING else to wear so I had to borrow your blue shirt but I'm renting it not borrowing it so here's ten bucks. I'll dry-clean it and everything.

Love,

Jackie

P.S. If you cut the butt out of my jeans you'll never see your shirt again.

I snorted and tossed the note back onto the coffee table, tucking the ten into my pocket. I had to hand it to Jackie; she was creative.

I flipped through channels, but I couldn't concentrate on anything. My brain wouldn't stop running through the events of the day in a torturous loop. Finally, I gave up and went to bed.

※

I slept horribly that night. I dreamed th   I'd gotten Ruby's boyfriend put in jail for selling drugs, but it wasn't Kenneth; it was some high school guy. I saw her at school, and she was standing outside of class, crying. She wouldn't talk to me.

When I woke in the morning, it took a few moments to realize it hadn't actually happened. But I had a heavy, ill taste in my mouth. And I knew with clarity how Ruby was feeling: totally betrayed.

The worst part was that I didn't blame her. In a way I *had* betrayed her. I would be furious, too, if someone interfered with my boyfriend.

I grabbed the cordless and called her. Then again ten minutes later. And again. I didn't care if she knew I was stalking her; she was my best friend, and *that* was why I'd gone through this weird piece of hell—to protect her.

I finally left a voice mail. "Ruby, I'm sorry. I should have told you what I was going to do. But I was worried that you'd stop me, and I was scared for you. I know you think it was sexy what he was doing, but it scared me, okay? Can you please call me?"

Of course she didn't call back.

I made coffee, but I only managed to drink a little bit. I didn't know how I'd get through school. But I'd already cut the day before; I couldn't let my grades slip two weeks before graduation. I pulled my hair into a ponytail, put on my most comfortable sweats and T-shirt, and faced another day at Mishawaka High.

Ruby didn't cut, either. I was on my way to first period when I heard heels tapping behind me. Ruby was the only person, possibly ever, who wore heels to our high school. I whipped

around. She swept past me, no intention of stopping. "Ruby!"
I called.

She kept going.

I walked fast to catch up.

"Stella, you're making this awkward." It was the calm
disdain in her voice that did me in. There was no anger, just the
disgust she reserved for people like Rhetta and Emma.

My voice came out higher than I intended, pleading. "Did
you get my message? I was trying to protect you."

"Yeah, so you said." Ruby pushed open the door of Mrs.
Leland's class. "Now, can you stop calling my cell?" She didn't
wait for an answer.

I stood stunned in the doorway.

"Excuse me." The words were loaded with poison that only
Rhetta was capable of.

I moved aside quickly, and she and Lisa walked in. *It's like
a convention of people who hate me,* I thought bitterly. If I was
leaving for college somewhere, I wouldn't care. But my whole
miserable future was tied up in this hostile little town.

A blackness descended on my soul. I hadn't felt like that in
a long time—not since I was in elementary school and processing Papi leaving. It was a choking, tight, hopeless feeling.

Trapped.

Chapter Thirty-one

For the next week I spent time in only three places: school, in front of the TV, and in bed.

The house seemed to visibly disintegrate around me, going from "sort of messy" to "filthy pigsty" in a matter of days. The trash sent out waves of stench so strong you could lean against them. Marcus spilled a box of cereal in the living room and walked in it, crunching pink dust into the carpet. Jackie's clothes migrated all over the house, hanging on doorknobs, folded over chairs, or dropped on the floor like garbage.

I watched with strange detachment. It wasn't that I was unwilling to help; it was that I *couldn't*.

Anybody who thinks depression is glamorous needs a slap.

Life felt like a big, fat nothing; and I felt like an even bigger, fatter nothing. I was too scared of ending up like my dad to even try to self-medicate.

So other than going to school, I vegged out, endlessly

examining the fact that within a year I had gone from universally well liked to universally despised. I decided there was no way I was going to graduation. What for? So Rhetta, Emma, and company could carry out whatever evil plot they had planned?

Not worth it.

I knew my mom would flip out (I was the first person in my family to be graduating from high school and was therefore considered a prodigy by all my aunts and uncles), so I figured I'd wait and break the news right before the ceremony. There would be less time for arguing that way. I also had this irrational fear that my mom would somehow *make* me walk if I gave her enough warning.

The days plodded by. On Ruby's birthday, when we had planned to party all night at Heartland, she didn't come to school. I was relieved. It would have been too awkward to see her with both of us aware of the fun we should have been having—if I hadn't done what I did.

I finished finals and went to the anticlimactic last day of school. It was as if I'd been swallowed by a social vortex: people ignored me and I ignored people. Unpopularity is contagious. I tried not to let it bother me, but inside I was shrinking into the fetal position.

I wasn't sure what I'd do without school and studying to fill the hours. Watch more TV?

But something happened after that last day of school that shook me out of my rut. When I got home in the afternoon, I was shocked to find the kitchen clean. Not just tidy, but counters-bleached clean. I felt a stab of guilt. Working constant doubles, Mom barely had time to eat and catch up on rest, let alone tackle the kitchen.

I opened the fridge. She'd gone shopping, too. It had to be done; we were down to bare-bones ramen-and-toast dinners. The shelves were stocked with lunch meat, juice, fruit, yogurt, and way more diet soda than I'd expect, considering Mom thought aspartame was the devil. She must have known I needed a treat. But how had she found the time to step up like this? And she hadn't nagged me once.

Pi rubbed against my leg, meowing; and I opened one of the new packs of sliced turkey and gave him a piece. Then I picked up the Comet and a scrubber. If Mom could do the kitchen, I could do the bathroom.

During the week that followed, between Mom and me, we got the house back in shape. I didn't like admitting it, but it felt good to be productive again. Plus, I was starting to feel better now that I didn't have to face people at school every day.

I still had no clue what to do with my dead-end life, though. It gnawed at me. I would have to get a job and apply next year to IUSB, St. Mary's, and Valparaiso—in other words, thug school, Catholic-girl-not-smart-enough-to-get-into-ND school, and farm school. Somebody had once called IUSB thirteenth grade, and that was how I felt about all three of them. But I didn't think I had any other options.

Meanwhile, commencement kept creeping toward me, one day at a time. My stress ratcheted up by fifty degrees when Mom came home from work one afternoon with a new dress from Ross. Mom *never* wore dresses.

"Look what I got," she said, pulling it out of the plastic bag. She held it against her body, looking almost shy. It was calf length, dark blue Lycra-acetate, with little diamond buttons. Totally nerdy, and totally endearing.

"Oh, Mom." I teared up. I'd been doing that a lot lately.

"Let me see," Jackie called. She came out of the laundry room, carrying a load of pinkish whites. "Hot damn!" she yelled, and shut her eyes like she was fainting from Mom's beauty.

"Jackie! Don't use that language!" Mom warned, but she was laughing. "I thought Stella's graduation deserved a special outfit. I'm going to hang it up."

"You don't have to, that stuff never wrinkles," Jackie called after her; but Mom was already on her way up the stairs.

I grimaced. Guilty was an understatement.

Jackie dumped the laundry on the floor and started sifting through it, separating her clothes from Marcus's.

It struck me, suddenly, how weird that was. "You did the laundry?"

"You don't have to sound so surprised." Jackie shook out one of Marcus's T-shirts. It was very definitely a pale rose color. "It's not like I haven't been doing everything around here."

It took a minute for her meaning to sink in. "The kitchen?"

She nodded.

"The grocery shopping?"

Another nod, and now a smug look.

"The garbage and the downstairs bathroom . . ."

A beaming smile. "Yas'm."

I gaped at her. "So that's why we have all that diet Dr. Pepper and Oreos. I thought Mom was being really cool."

"Well, you checked out of life, so somebody had to step in. The house was starting to stink." Jackie paused. "Mom said you only applied to Notre Dame because you thought you had to stay here and take care of us. You don't, okay? I got it covered."

She said it so gently that my breath caught. After a moment I said, "You rock, Jackie."

"I know." She studied me. "Are you going to be okay? You've been so weird lately."

"I'm doing better. There are just these girls at school. And Ruby's mad at me about . . . this thing. And I feel like a total loser for not going to college next year. I'm going to have to work at the gas station or something." I meant it as a joke, but it didn't sound like one.

Jackie put on her tough love face—she can be so much like Mom. "No, what you need to do is find something awesome to do next year. And in the fall you need to apply to all kinds of colleges *away from South Bend.*"

Looking at Jackie folding laundry, for the first time I began to believe it was a possibility. But I wasn't ready to talk about that part yet. Instead I said, "What cool thing could I do? Ruby said I should do something that would look good on college applications, but I don't even know what that would be."

"Go volunteer somewhere," Jackie said immediately. "Colleges love that stuff. And you'd be good at it. You're always trying to help people, anyway. Look at Ruby, and look how you're always up in my grill. You *want* to help people."

I giggled. "There's the Salvation Army on Michigan Avenue."

"I think you should do it somewhere out of South Bend," Jackie said firmly. "You need to get out of here, Stella, and you need to realize we're going to be cool without you. I mean, that way DaShawn can move into your bedroom, and we can turn the house into Blood headquarters. . . ."

It took me a second to laugh; but when I did, it was the

snorting kind. My little sister was here this whole time and yet I almost didn't know her.

In my heart, I recognized the rightness of her words. I did need to leave South Bend. And I did like to help people. I'd thought before of going into social work of some kind; this could be like a trial run. I didn't have to go far—Chicago was only two hours away—but I did need something of my own, a new start.

Possibilities flooded my mind: an internship, maybe something where I could live at the place. Definitely working with women and children, because that's what I knew best, what I'd been doing all my life, really.

I couldn't wait to get to the library and go online. It had been a long time since I'd had a sense of purpose, and it lifted me like a kite.

I got off the couch and grabbed my sister in an impulsive hug. "Thanks, Jackie," I said.

"It's all good," she said, hugging me back.

Chapter Thirty-two

Mom did not take the news about commencement well. When she crosses herself and says "Lord have mercy" instead of screaming, you know it's *really* bad. I waited too long to tell her.

Way too long.

But you know that feeling when things snowball and you feel paralyzed? That's what the few days before commencement were like: I watched Mom try on different shoes with her new dress, get her shift covered at work, and talk about Sizzler versus Friday's for a celebration dinner. The whole time I kept thinking I would find the right moment to break the news, but it never came; and finally it was the actual day of the ceremony.

When Mom started putting on makeup—which she never does—a cold, bad feeling grew in my gut; and I knew I'd screwed up by letting it get this far. I blurted, "I decided I'm not going to walk."

Mom's hand holding her lipstick froze. "What?"

Words tumbled out: "I wanted to tell you earlier, but I knew you'd be mad. It's fine; they'll mail me the diploma, and it won't affect my record or anything. We can still get dressed up and go to dinner."

That's when Mom crossed herself and said, "Lord have mercy." Then she turned to me with fire in her eyes. "Stella, what kind of nonsense are you talking about? This is your high school graduation!"

"I don't want to walk. It's just a ceremony. It doesn't mean anything."

Mom's ears turned red. "It is *not* just a ceremony. It's a life event. It's . . . you're the first Chavez to graduate high school— and you don't, you don't want to celebrate that?" She was so upset she was stuttering.

I realized I had to tell her. "Mom, there are these girls that hate me." I struggled to keep my voice even. It was hard to talk about it. "They said if I go to graduation they're going to do something horrible. And I can't deal with it right now. I don't have anybody to hang out with before or after. Beth and Christine stopped being my friends a long time ago, and now Ruby is mad at me, too. I just can't face it alone."

Mom looked stunned. "Oh, honey. Why didn't you tell me?"

"I don't know," I said.

"Come on. We need to sit down." Mom pulled me by the hand to the living room and led me to the couch.

Jackie peeked out of the kitchen holding a liter of diet soda. Clearly she'd been swigging from the bottle again. "What's going on? Why do you guys look all serious?"

"We need a minute to talk, Jackie," Mom said.

"It's okay. She can stay." I surprised myself and Jackie, but I meant it.

Jackie came and sat on my other side, a mom-sister sandwich. They both looked almost comically concerned. "What's wrong?"

I told them, giving details this time—just about the picture, not Kenneth. It felt so good to see Mom's fierceness and Jackie's fury as the story unfolded.

"I'm calling DaShawn," Jackie announced when I was done. "You can hang with his crew before and after, and nobody will mess with you, believe me. He thinks you're cool, anyway."

The idea was so preposterous that I laughed.

"What? Don't be a snob. DaShawn is good people. And his girl, Jen, is like the hardest chick at Morrison, and she'll be there. If DaShawn tells her, she'll handle Rhetta and Emma."

"Wait, his girl?" I echoed. I had been so positive that he and Jackie had a thing.

Jackie rolled her eyes. "For the five-hundredth time, *DaShawn and I are just friends.*"

"How come you didn't tell me he had a girlfriend?"

"Um, I don't know. Maybe because you wouldn't have believed me?"

A grin split my face. "What do you mean? I always believe you."

"Sure you do. Just like you believed I wasn't messing with gangs. Remember that fake tat you were tripping on? It's an anarchy sign. Anarchists don't join organizations, and a *gang* is an *organization*, genius."

Mom gave Jackie a sharp look. "You said it was a boy's initial."

Jackie looked a little ashamed. "Sorry. I was just mad you guys were on my back about it."

I stared at Jackie, not sure whether to laugh or shake my head. I wasn't so sure anarchy was better than gang membership; but given everything that had unfolded in the past couple weeks, I wasn't really worried about her anymore.

And it felt amazing.

Mom sighed. "Oh, Jackie." Then she turned to me and said firmly, "Even if you have to stand the whole time by yourself, I think you should go, Stella. There will be plenty of teacher supervision, and we'll meet you the minute you walk offstage. Don't let these girls take this away from you. Graduation is not about parties and friends—not in our family. It's bigger than that. You're walking for Nana and Papa, because they never had a chance to go to high school. You're walking for me and your dad—we didn't know what we were giving up until it was too late. And you're walking for Jackie and Marcus so they can follow in your footsteps." Mom's blue eyes were more serious than I'd ever seen them.

As if on cue, Marcus wandered into the living room, skateboard under his arm. His hair was flopping in his eyes, and he looked vulnerable and tough at the same time in his baggy jeans and ancient Savers shirt. He would be in junior high next year. I couldn't believe it. "What are you guys doing? Are we going to Stella's thing or what?"

Mom and Jackie looked at me.

"Yeah," I said finally. "Just let me get dressed."

It didn't take long: I pulled on my favorite green dress and slid into comfortable low heels. A little makeup, a brush through my hair, and I was ready. Mom and Jackie had finished getting ready, too, and were waiting in the living room. As for Marcus, we were happy he was at least wearing clean shoes.

When I came out, Mom faked an embarrassing wolf whistle.

"Stop," I said. "Let's just get this over with."

Mom's eyes were twinkling. "Wait, that dress is missing something." She held out her hand and light reflected off royal-blue stones.

I gasped. "I can wear it?" It was Nana's sapphire necklace, the only real piece of jewelry Mom owned. She had never let me or Jackie borrow it before, even though we'd begged a million times.

In answer, Mom fastened it around my neck. There is something about wearing real jewelry: I stood straighter, felt almost beautiful.

"Wait, me, too." Jackie dashed to her room and came back with her prized bottle of J'Adore, sixty-dollar department store perfume that she guarded like a dragon. Smiling, she spritzed a little on my collarbone and wrists.

Marcus hightailed it into the den and emerged a minute later clutching his good-luck Spider-Man key chain. It had been his talisman since the first day of kindergarten, when Mom had told him he could take one friend to school. He frowned, daring me to laugh.

I took it solemnly and said, "Thank you. I'll hold it the whole time."

Mom pushed open the door and stood aside to let us pass. "Okay, kiddos. Let's go."

Wearing jewelry fit for a queen, smelling good, and strangely comforted by the red plastic figure in my hand, I walked down the steps and got into the car.

Chapter Thirty-three

Whatever confidence I'd possessed evaporated when we got to the auditorium and had to separate. My family headed for the bleachers, and I went to the big conference room behind the backstage area, where everyone was supposed to line up and walk out on cue to receive their diplomas.

With half an hour to go, nobody was in line yet, and it was deafening and hot in there; a crowd of black robes and moving tassels. I tugged on my cap and gown, hoping it would give me some anonymity.

Doubt and anxiety were creeping up like evil twins. Every dark-haired girl looked like Rhetta; every blonde looked like Emma or Stacy. I decided if I drifted around, never staying in one place for too long, I'd be harder to spot.

Unfortunately, this worked for about fifteen minutes. Then I "drifted" right into Stacy.

Her eyes widened, and she turned and hissed, "She's here!"

I tried to get away, but the crowd was thick. Rhetta, Emma, Stacy, and Brianna closed around me. I took a breath and squeezed Spider-Man.

"I thought we told you not to show up," Emma said loudly.

Brianna elbowed her, glancing at Mrs. Leland, who was about twenty feet away, trying to keep order.

Emma lowered her voice. "So what the fuck are you doing here?"

I stared at her, weighing my options, noting how close Mrs. Leland was. I would not break. There was nothing they could do to me here but talk.

"Answer her," Stacy said.

I didn't move.

"What are you, stoned?" Rhetta sneered. "Like your loser dad?"

That hurt like the slice of a knife. Rhetta had lived in South Bend forever. Like all of us old-timers, she knew more about everybody's family life than she should. But I couldn't believe she'd drag that out.

"Is her dad a stoner, too?" Emma asked with interest. Emma was a transplant.

Rhetta eyed me. "Oh, yeah. He's a junkie. He used to stand out by Lowe's with one of those signs, you know? He totally fucked up my dad's fence."

I felt dead inside suddenly, like Rhetta's words had vacuumed all the air and feeling out of me. Then the ever-shifting crowd moved, and Christine and Beth walked past. I saw Christine's quick eyes take everything in.

"Her dad was twitchy; you know how junkies are." Rhetta

shook her wrists, sending her hands fluttering. "Gotta . . . get . . . my . . . fix."

Christine stopped. Beth looked horrified.

"What are *you* looking at?" Rhetta challenged.

I'm not sure if Christine was going to answer. But she didn't get a chance, because a bigger distraction started just a few feet away.

"There's a mistake on your list, then!" said a loud, defiant voice.

It was Ruby, I realized with shock. She was standing by the double doors, wearing a tight red dress with impossible heels. A shimmery scarf was tied around her shoulders, covering the lines on her chest. Her hands were on her hips, and she was facing Mrs. Leland.

"I'm afraid your dress . . . didn't you get the flyer, dear? You need a cap and gown to walk." Mrs. Leland had never known how to deal with Ruby, I thought.

"I can't afford a cap and gown. Do you want a lawsuit about economic discrimination?" Ruby's shoulders were squared, her eyes spitting fire. I was transported back to the first time I saw her, fighting about the dress code in a different way.

Mrs. Leland coughed nervously. "No, of course not. But we don't have your diploma ready, because you're not on the list, so I'm afraid—"

"I don't care. You can give me a piece of binder paper. I just want to walk. It's a *rite of passage*," Ruby said, using Leland's own words against her.

Mrs. Leland's eyes darted around for help. "Let me discuss this with Mr. Montoya. I'm not sure about protocol for this type of situation." She disappeared out the door, and Ruby's eyes met mine, then skimmed the girls around me. Face unreadable, she turned and followed Leland out of the room.

"Your friend looks even skankier than usual," Emma remarked.

"Is she seriously too poor to rent a cap and gown? Did her sugar daddy dump her or something?" said Brianna.

"Actually, *she's* the poor one," Rhetta said smugly, looking at me. "Why do you think she doesn't have a cellie?"

Beth flushed. "Stop it!"

It was as if she hadn't spoken. Rhetta's eyes stayed on mine. "Maybe you can do fences like your dad, save up, and get a phone."

Somehow I kept my face under control, but I was crumpling on the inside. I never should have come. The image of Papi doing Rhetta's dad's fence tightened my chest, burned my eyes. All I wanted was to escape before they saw me cry.

I tried to push past Rhetta, but she stepped closer to Stacy, blocking me.

Then, behind Emma, I saw Ruby come back into the room. She walked purposefully toward us. I took a shaky breath as she shouldered between Emma and Stacy and joined our little circle with a smile.

"Hey, what are you guys talking about?" Ruby's face was open and friendly, her tone sweet.

Everyone looked at her in shock.

Rhetta recovered quickly: "Just wondering why you bitches showed up."

Ruby's eyes widened. "Rhetta Nakamura, what are you talking about?"

"Are you high? I'm talking about the fact that we told

you not to show your slutty asses at our graduation."

"That's a mean thing to say. We're graduating, too." Ruby's voice was cringing and submissive, but she was smiling oddly. I felt a spark of hope. She was running some kind of game.

"Why? Do you need a high school diploma to work in a strip bar?" Emma asked.

"Rhetta, Emma, Stacy, and Brianna, why can't you guys just leave us alone? We're tired of you always picking on us," Ruby whined pathetically. But she stepped right up into Emma's face with a wicked grin.

"Get out of my face, you trashy bitch, unless you want your ass kicked now instead of later," Emma snapped.

"Oh my gosh, Emma Hausbeck! I can't believe you just said that!" Ruby squealed with delight.

At that moment Mrs. DeVries stormed through the door. She swiveled until she spotted us and then literally pushed students out of her way to get to us. Something small, black, and plastic clattered to the floor. It looked like a Bluetooth.

"What's *that*?" Ruby asked in mock surprise.

We all stared down, confused. Emma was the first to understand. Her face went white. "Is that the mic?" she said in horror.

DeVries swooped into the circle and snatched the mic from the floor, fumbling for the OFF button. She was trembling. "How did this get back here?"

"She brought it!" Rhetta said immediately, pointing at Ruby.

"I found it on the stage floor. I thought somebody lost their iPod headset. I didn't even know what it was," Ruby said, eyes huge. "They were saying all this mean stuff to us. Did everybody in the audience hear that? Did our *families* hear that?"

Rhetta looked sick. I suddenly remembered her mentioning in Leland's class that her grandparents were coming all the way from Japan to see her graduate.

DeVries shoved the headset into her suit pocket. "All of you, come with me now."

"But Mrs. DeVries, they're supposed to start calling names in a few minutes. I didn't do anything wrong," Ruby said. "My last name starts with *C,* so I'll be in the beginning. Stella, too."

Christine spoke up. "Stella and Ruby didn't do anything." She tilted her head toward the others. "They were the ones saying stuff."

"Yeah," said Beth. "Didn't you hear them?"

DeVries took a deep breath. Her cheeks were bright red. "Fine. Rhetta, Emma, Stacy, Brianna, follow me."

"But—" began Rhetta.

"No! Not a word!" DeVries almost shrieked. "Now!"

Ruby waited until DeVries had turned, then gave a delicate wave as the girls walked away.

Our eyes met in a moment of ecstatic triumph. Had she seriously just pulled that off?

"That was amazing," I whispered.

Ruby's eyes were dancing. "Did you see Rhetta's face?"

"That's why you kept saying their names," I marveled. "I thought you were being so weird."

From my periphery I could see Christine and Beth moving away. I turned quickly. "You guys, wait. Please don't go. I'm—" I felt myself blushing. I didn't know how to express how much

I loved them at that moment. "I can't believe you did that. Thank you."

"It was no big deal," Christine said, looking away.

"Yes, it was," I insisted.

"It was," Ruby affirmed.

Beth smiled at Ruby, for the first time, I think.

"We should go. Everybody is getting in line," said Christine.

"Will you guys meet me after?" I asked awkwardly.

Beth and Christine glanced at each other. "If you want to," said Beth.

"I want to," I said so fervently that Christine smiled. I hadn't seen that in so long. Impulsively, I gave her a hug. Christine wasn't a hugger, and she felt like a board in my arms. But when I pulled away, she was still smiling.

"I thought you were going to kiss me there," she quipped.

"Maybe I should have," I said.

Christine was laughing as she walked away.

"We should get in line, too," said Ruby. "How many people do you think there are between Caroline and Chavez?"

"Not many. Do you really get to walk without the cap and gown?"

Ruby grinned. "Mr. Montoya said I could. He has a soft spot for poor kids."

I shook my head, amazed. "That's a hot dress. You look beautiful."

"I bought it myself," Ruby said with emphasis.

We looked at each other, and I asked a question with my eyes.

"I talked to the Sharifs," she said. "I get that you were trying to help me, okay?"

I nodded.

"I dumped him."

My heart swelled with relief, delight, and so many other good feelings I couldn't separate them all.

"I was really mad that you interfered, but then I realized you're the only person that ever cared enough to do that. So . . ." Ruby shrugged. "I forgive you."

I laughed out loud. "Thank you very much, Your Highness."

"Well, what do you want? A medal?"

"Nah. What you just did was pretty good."

And we linked arms and walked out the door to go graduate.

Mrs. Leland fluttered through the dark backstage area, helping stragglers find their places and imploring people to *shhhhh*. Apparently we were already behind schedule. Outside, we heard the audience fall quiet.

Then Mr. Montoya's voice boomed out: "Hello, everyone. Welcome to a very special day, Mishawaka High School Commencement. Before we begin, I want to apologize for the unfortunate incident a few minutes ago. There was a mix-up with the microphone, and you heard some students being very cruel and inappropriate. I want you to know that we do not tolerate that kind of behavior at Mishawaka High. There will be disciplinary action taken. And now, let's put this behind us and move on with the wonderful ceremony celebrating our GRADUATING MISHAWAKA COUGARS!" *Clap clap clap . . .*

Ruby and I exchanged delighted looks.

After a couple of cheesy speeches from the debate coach and the football coach, the band broke into a shaky rendition of our fight song, which was really just a rip-off of the Fighting Irish with a few chords changed and a lot less musical talent.

"When I call your name, step forward, shake hands, take the diploma," Mr. Montoya said in the general direction of backstage.

"They already learned that in rehearsal," hissed De Vries, but the mic caught her voice and broadcast it over the auditorium. There was a ripple of laughter.

Finally Mr. Montoya began to call names.

We had only a couple hundred kids in my class, and it wasn't long before Montoya got through the As and Bs. With every kid that walked, catcalls, whistles, and claps exploded from a different corner of the audience. We were starting the Cs, and a thought hit me. Would anybody clap for Ruby? Would they boo?

"Is Gina here?" I asked Ruby.

"Of course not. I didn't even tell her about it."

I frowned. "Then why did you come? Just to get back at Rhetta and them?"

Ruby looked at me like I might be slow. "I came for you. Because I didn't want you dealing with them alone. Getting hold of the mic was something I figured out at the last minute, when I saw them messing with you."

"How did you do it?"

Ruby shrugged. "It was easy. It was sitting on the podium where it always is for assemblies, and the curtain was still closed. I just took it and turned it on."

"David Calloway," called Montoya. The kid in front of us disappeared onstage.

"Ruby Caroline."

Ruby threw back her shoulders and walked onstage. I peeked through the curtain and held my breath. She looked incredible in that crazy dress, clicking across the stage like a rock star. Montoya winked at her and handed her a piece of binder paper. A piercing whistle cut the air, along with some claps and "GO, RUBY! GO, RUBY!"

It was my family. Mom and Jackie were screaming and clapping, and Marcus was blowing this orange whistle that was as loud as an air-raid siren. Tears filled my eyes, and Dana Chilberg, who was standing behind me, had to gently shove me onstage when Montoya called my name.

When my hand closed over my diploma, it was the same thing all over again, with Mom and Jackie and Marcus going nuts. I looked right at them and mouthed "I love you." I didn't care who saw. Then I walked down the stage and took my place next to Ruby in the folding chairs reserved for graduates.

Her eyes were suspiciously shiny, but I knew better than to say anything.

"Nice diploma," I told her.

Ruby looked down at the binder paper in her lap. "I'm definitely framing it." She turned it so I could see.

To Ruby, a girl with a lot of spunk. Good luck. You're going to take the rest of your life by storm. Your diploma will be in the mail.
David Montoya

We both burst out giggling. It was the perfect beginning for the rest of our lives.